"Don't," She
Pul

Greg didn't say a word, but his fingers
tightened and refused to release her. She was
dragged against him, struggling, and his head
came down to shut out the light.

For one more second Dinah resisted the
heated pressure of his lips, then she weakly
surrendered, the blood beating in her ears and
deafening her. Her hands lay against his hard
chest, the heavy thud of his heart beating
under her palms. She had lost the ability to
think. She was melting, burning, her mouth
crushed under that hard, fierce demand.

Greg pulled back with a long, harsh intake of
breath. His face was very flushed. . . .

"That's more like it," he said huskily, grimly
satisfied.

LAURA HARDY
has five children ranging in age from six through
eighteen. She and her family live on the Isle of
Man off the northwest coast of England.

Dear Reader:

At Silhouette we try to publish books with you, our reader, in mind, and we're always trying to think of something new. We're very pleased to announce the creation of Silhouette First Love, a new line of contemporary romances written by the very finest young adult writers especially for our twelve-to-sixteen-year-old readers. First Love has many of the same elements you've enjoyed in Silhouette Romances—love stories, happy endings and the same attention to detail and description—but features heroines and situations with which our younger readers can more easily identify.

First Love from Silhouette will be available in bookstores this October. We will introduce First Love with six books, and each month thereafter we'll bring you two new First Love romances.

We welcome any suggestions or comments, and I invite you to write to us at the address below.

Karen Solem
Editor-in-Chief
Silhouette Books
P.O. Box 769
New York, N.Y. 10019

LAURA HARDY
Playing with Fire

Silhouette *Romance*

Published by Silhouette Books New York

America's Publisher of Contemporary Romance

Other Silhouette Romances by Laura Hardy

Burning Memories

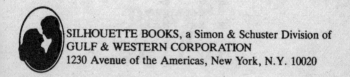

SILHOUETTE BOOKS, a Simon & Schuster Division of
GULF & WESTERN CORPORATION
1230 Avenue of the Americas, New York, N.Y. 10020

Copyright © 1981 by Laura Hardy

Distributed by Pocket Books

ISBN: 0-671-57101-X

First Silhouette printing September, 1981

10 9 8 7 6 5 4 3 2 1

America's Publisher of Contemporary Romance

Printed in the U.S.A.

Playing
with Fire

Chapter One

A stranger might be forgiven for thinking he had wandered into a luxury hotel rather than an office block, Dinah thought as she pushed through the swinging doors after a bewildered man who stopped dead, almost tripping her up, to look around him in disbelief.

The ultramodern reception area was crowded with tubular steel tubs which held tropical plants, their dark green leaves and curling fronds transforming the cool ceramic walls and floor into an indoor garden. A metallic fountain played gently among them, sprinkling everyone who passed with cool drops of water. The staff constantly complained about it, but the designer had been given some sort of award for his work on the complex, and Sir Gee wasn't moving that fountain for anyone.

"Cost me a bomb," he always said with satisfaction.

Sir George Randal equated cost with value. "I paid through the nose for it and it stays."

"You can get soaked to the skin just walking through the foyer," Dinah had pointed out, and he had given her his crocodile smile.

"Tell them to buy umbrellas if they're so afraid of getting wet."

Dinah had not laughed. Now, as she skirted the bemused stranger, she wondered if she ought to tell him to buy an umbrella. His gaze fixed on the fountain, his dark brows lifted in sheer open incredulity.

"What on earth is that?" Dinah heard him mutter. Before the modernization this had been a perfectly recognizable office block. Most of the space now given to what the staff called, among themselves, the jungle had been in functional use. Now it was just a space to trek across before one reached the lifts, but as Dinah began to make her way through the jungle her arm was caught. Surprised, she looked around with a coolly polite expression.

"Yes?"

"What's all this? What genius thought that thing up?" The voice was deep and derisive as he gestured toward the fountain. Dinah's glance skated over the face, registering a brief impression of good looks, but she did not have time to chat with strangers, however attractive.

"You'll find the receptionist over there, sir," she told him, detaching herself and walking away.

"Thank you," he said to her departing back, his tone dry, and she heard him walking behind her, his footsteps ringing on the tiled floor in the direction of the reception desk.

An elegant young woman in pale gray sat under a line of modernistic prints whose swirl of black dots reminded Dinah of fingerprints. Her smooth enameled face was unbroken by any sign of life. It was rumored that she had come with the fountain. She sat there all day gazing blankly across the tropical plants as though waiting for Tarzan to swing out of them.

As Dinah neared the lifts one of them opened with a smooth swish. She put on a sudden spurt and slid into it just as the doors closed again. Through them as they shut she caught sight of the stranger's face and got a hard look from his gray eyes, without feeling particularly bothered. She was in a hurry. From the casual way he had been sauntering into the building she got the feeling he was in no hurry at all.

Examining herself briefly in the corner mirror, she saw that her silk shirt had worked itself out of the waistband of her cream suit. Tucking it back in, Dinah made a face at herself. Sir Gee was obsessive about tiny details. He noticed the slightest things, even if she had a hair out of place, and she made sure she never did. Tall and slender, Dinah wore her blond hair drawn back off her face and fastened in a French knot at the back of her head, the classic hairstyle lending clarity to the oval outline of her features. Most men, looking into her widely spaced blue eyes, missed the glint of amusement in them. Dinah's calm manner generally hid her sense of humor.

The phone was ringing as she reached the office. She decided to ignore it. The room was fresh and cool, the windows wide open letting in a cool, refreshing breeze. But Dinah went over to close them. Every morning the cleaners opened them, and every morning Dinah had to shut them before Sir Gee arrived and burst out furiously, "Who opened the bloody window?" He regarded fresh air as dangerous stuff and lived in a constant reek of cigar smoke.

Standing by her desk, she flipped through the post. The phone went on ringing. The patient, persistent shrillness didn't bother Dinah. She was used to it. The phone rang all day and half the time the calls weren't important.

Sir Gee would be here soon and he would expect to have his mail waiting for him on his desk. He kept strict hours and expected everyone else to do the same. Work was a religion with him. Everything had to be done just right and on time. He had been born in the lap of luxury, but his nature inclined him toward a fanatic belief in working flat out.

Sir Gee had a low frustration threshold. He liked his own way and he liked it at once. His favorite phrase was: "I don't like it, I won't have it." Having been born with a silver spoon in his mouth had left him with the distinct impression that the world was duty bound to fall in with his wishes. Most of the people around him were, in fact, only too happy to do so, which increased his belief that he had the right idea. Dinah was fond of him, but she saw him as a large pink baby in his expensively tailored Savile Row suits, his roars of rage only convincing her that the world was his playpen.

Having sorted through the mail, she picked up the phone at last. "Sir George Randal's office." The cool, modulated voice changed as she heard the voice at the other end. "Oh, hello, Dilly." Warily she shifted, her slim hip resting against the desk. "Something up?"

"I can't make it for lunch today," Dilly said breathlessly. "Sorry, Dinah."

"Have you got to work through your lunch break?" Dinah asked in surprise.

"Hamish is in town." Dilly's voice took on a defiant ring. She knew what Dinah's reaction would be, and she was right.

"Oh, Dilly, you're crazy if you start seeing him again!"

Dilly responded with trembling fury. "You've never liked Hamish. You're always demeaning him. Mind your own business." The phone crashed down at the other end and Dinah sighed, slowly replacing her own receiver. When would Dilly learn some sense? Hamish was nothing but a headache to her. All Dilly ever got out of that relationship was trouble, but she was a glutton for punishment. However badly Hamish treated her, she ran after him the minute he whistled. It didn't make sense to Dinah. Dinah's pride would never take treatment like that.

She laid the opened mail on Sir Gee's desk, glancing around the room. At this hour of the morning it was immaculate, the air clear of cigar smoke, the desk tidy. It wouldn't stay that way for long. Sir Gee exploded into rooms like a cloud of atomic dust.

The door swung open then and she turned, her smile vanishing as she recognized the man who had been so amazed by the new reception area. His gray eyes were viewing her with narrowed interest, and Dinah stiffened at the slow head-to-foot appraisal he was giving her.

"Can I help you?" she demanded in her coldest voice.

"Isn't he here yet?" He glanced at his watch with exaggerated amazement. "Late? My heavens, is the world crumbling?"

"Sir George will be here soon. May I ask if you have an appointment, sir . . . ?" She had glanced at the diary only a moment ago and she didn't recall any appointments for this hour. Sir Gee liked to keep the first hour of the day free for office routine.

"No," the attractive stranger drawled, smiling. "I haven't got an appointment."

"Then I'm afraid . . ."

Ignoring her, he walked past and took up a casual position on the edge of Sir Gee's desk, one long leg swinging.

Dinah prickled with annoyance. Who did he think he was? If Sir Gee walked in and found this man lounging on his desk as if he owned the place, he would flip his lid.

"Please don't sit on Sir George's desk," she said icily. The stranger gave her a mocking grin and picked up the mail, sifting through it, running an eye over the top letters.

"How dare you?" Dinah burst out, shooting forward to snatch the pile from him. "Would you mind leaving this office?"

Leaning back, he stared down into her wide, angry blue eyes. "What's your name?"

"Please leave this office," she repeated, a little red coin in each cheek.

"You'll blow a fuse if you're not careful," he told her without budging an inch. It infuriated her further that he murmured that in a deep, amused voice.

With a struggle she retrieved her usual calm. "Look, Mr. . . . ?"

He surveyed her through half-lowered lids. "If you won't tell me your name why should I tell you mine?"

She knew he was laughing at her and she didn't like it. He was a very tall, lean man with a toughly modeled face, the lines of it giving an impression of power rather than good looks until he smiled. His mouth in repose was hard and controlled, but when it curled up in a smile it took on a warmth which altered his whole expression.

Now that she took a closer look at him she realized that, whoever he was, he must have money. That dark, formal suit was expensively tailored, although he wore it with a casual panache which indicated that he didn't care how much it had cost. He wore his jacket open, his tie loosely knotted, his blue-and-white-striped shirt open at the collar. Dinah got an impression of total ease, lazy amusement, and her blue eyes iced over. Something about him antagonized her.

It might have been the equally interested scrutiny she was getting from him. He was running his eyes down over her from her smooth blond head to her elegantly shod feet, and he was taking his time about it, as though he were enjoying the view, making sure not to miss anything.

When the gray eyes lifted Dinah met them with a glare. "Very charming," he murmured, arching one dark brow.

Dinah said through her clenched teeth, "Why don't you leave your name and telephone number and I'll see that Sir George hears you want to see him."

13

"He's got you well trained, hasn't he?" Shifting back, he took another narrowed look at her. "How long have you worked for him?"

Dinah wondered if she ought to ring downstairs for the security men.

"What happened to the redhead?" he asked, tilting his head in lazy scrutiny as she warily moved around the desk with the intention of picking up the phone. What was security's number? She had never had to call them before. Strangers generally never got up to this level of the building.

She halted, uncertain, staring at him. What if he did know Sir George? Her predecessor *had* been a redhead, now that she thought of it.

"She left."

"Got married, did she?"

Dinah nodded and saw a nostalgic gleam in his eye. Dinah could imagine why. The girl had been very pretty.

"Pity," he said. "Now, *she* was a very welcoming girl."

Before Dinah could respond there was a noise like an invading army in the corridor. The stranger turned, smiling.

"Late?" he asked, as the door opened. "You'll have to go, you know. This just isn't good enough. Late twice in thirty years. What do you think you're doing?"

Sir Gee gave a strangled yelp. "Greg! I didn't expect you yet." He rolled forward and shook the stranger clumsily by the shoulders. "Nice to have you back home, m'boy!"

Dinah stared at them both, fixed on the spot in

horror. The truth clicked home to her. She should have realized before, but she had been too busy feeling angry with him for being so arrogant.

He gave her a sideways grin. "Introduce us, Father. She wanted to throw me out of the office—I think she suspected I was an industrial spy come to steal all the firm's secrets."

Sir Gee roared with laughter, taking in Dinah's flush. "Have you been teasing my Miss Trevor? Dinah, this is Greg, my son. I've told you about him, haven't I?"

Constantly, she thought, and why on earth didn't it occur to me before? But then, how was I to guess that Sir Gee's son looked like that? There wasn't a shred of resemblance between them. Greg Randal towered above his father, who was as wide as he was high, and the long-limbed power of Greg's body would never make anyone suspect his parentage.

Greg Randal held out his hand. Dinah politely gave him hers and withdrew it almost at once, feeling embarrassed.

Sir Gee had been talking about his son ever since she had started to work for him a year ago. She had known for months that Greg Randal was coming home. He had been in the States for two years, running that side of the firm's operations, but now he was taking over one of the top executive positions here in London. Why hadn't she put two and two together until now?

Hurriedly glancing at Sir Gee, she asked, "Would you like some coffee?"

"Good girl." Sir Gee nodded, and Dinah retreated to her own office in relief. She was glad to get away from the situation.

When she took the coffee through she found Sir Gee seated behind his desk, talking, while his son sprawled in a chair facing him, his long legs stretched out and his feet on the edge of the desk.

Dinah glided over to put down the coffee. Every step she took was watched by those lazy gray eyes. As she handed him his cup she saw his thick black lashes flick up and he gave her a long, amused look.

"Still feeling sore?"

"Of course not," Dinah said coolly. "I hope you enjoyed your little joke."

"Don't tease her," Sir Gee commanded, sipping his coffee. "He's a terrible tease, Dinah. Always looking for amusement. Take no notice of him."

"I won't," she said, and got another amused look before she withdrew again.

Sir Gee buzzed for her an hour later and told her to get Mrs. Murchison down. "Tell her Greg's here and wants to discuss some office arrangements with her."

Dinah said, "Yes, Sir George," and got Karen Murchison on the phone. Karen was a woman of thirty with a flat, calm voice and a level temperament. It didn't surprise her at all to be told that Greg Randal was back. "Right," she said. "I'll be down in a few minutes."

Sir George's first appointment arrived, and Dinah informed Sir Gee of the fact.

"Oh," said Sir Gee, sighing. "Well, show him in; Greg will have to use your office for a moment."

Dinah showed the new arrival through and Greg Randal strolled into her office, taking up a perch on the side of her desk. Didn't he like chairs? she thought as she sat down at her typewriter.

Fixing him with a pointed stare, she said, "You don't mind if I get on with my work?"

"Carry on," he invited.

Dinah deliberately looked at the spare chair. "Do sit down," she said sweetly.

"I'm comfortable where I am," he told her, and she gave a deep, carefully audible sigh.

"Surely you'd be more comfortable in a chair?"

"Ah, but then I wouldn't have such a good view of you," he said, his mouth curling up at the edges in that amused smile.

I am going to get tired of that smile, Dinah thought, looking away from it to the copy she was typing. He's a flirt, and that is one type of man I cannot stand. Those eyes issued an invitation every time they met her own, but Dinah wasn't interested. He wasn't her type at all. He was rather too sure of himself, rather too charming. She didn't trust all that charm.

Karen poked her head through the door and came in after it, holding out her hand. "Greg! Hello. Welcome home. How does it feel to be back? Chilly after the States?"

"Distinctly chilly," he murmured, glancing at Dinah sideways as he spoke.

Karen laughed. "But I bet that you're glad to be back. When did you get into London?"

"This morning," he said. "I'm in the office on a flying visit before I go down to Staunton. I just wanted to check with you that all the office arrangements have been made."

"You've got the staff you asked for," Karen said, smiling. "I shunted Tim Weston in from marketing and brought Jimmy down from the Liverpool office. He was extremely pleased and grateful. He was very homesick for London."

"What about a secretary?" he asked.

Karen shrugged. "Take your pick."

The black head swiveled and Dinah heard Karen laugh. "Not Dinah, of course," she told him. "Sir Gee wouldn't lose her for a fortune."

Dinah ignored them both, working with apparent concentration, her blond head bent.

"Pity," he said mournfully, watching her. "I enjoy having a blonde around the place."

"So does your father," Karen told him. "Shall I fix up some interviews for you or just pick one out?"

"I'll see a handful of them," Greg Randal decided. "I start work next week. Fix some interviews for Friday."

After a further brief exchange, Karen left and Dinah waited for Greg Randal to do the same. Instead, he came over to her desk and leaned over, his long hand lifting her chin.

Dinah bristled. "Yes?"

"Have lunch with me," he murmured, his dark head blotting out the sunlight.

"Sorry, I've got a lunch date," she lied.

"Break it," he proposed. "We'll eat somewhere really fantastic to celebrate."

"Celebrate what?" she asked before she had had time to stop herself from responding.

"My arrival back in London," he said, teasing her with those gray eyes.

"Sorry," Dinah said, trying to convey by her icy tone that she didn't regard that as anything to celebrate, at least not for her.

"It's hard work," he complained.

"What is?"

"Trying to break through your force field," he told her. "Do you ever switch it off?"

Dinah pulled her head out of his grip. "I've got work to do, Mr. Randal," she informed him tartly.

He shrugged, moving away. "See you soon, Dinah," he threatened silkily as he opened the door to leave.

Not if I see you first, Dinah decided as he closed it and she heard him cross the corridor to the elevator bank.

That afternoon, Sir Gee broke off some dictation to say, "Charmer, isn't he?"

Dinah looked at him blankly. What was he talking about?

"Greg," he said, with proud satisfaction. "A charmer, isn't he? Gets it from his mother."

Certainly not from you, thought Dinah. Sir Gee was a forceful, dynamic man with incredible amounts of energy and determination, but nobody in his right mind would describe him as a charmer.

"You know my wife," he said, looking at the large studio portrait which took pride of place on his cluttered desk. One of Sir Gee's most endearing qualities was his adoring devotion to his wife. He thought the world of her. He was right, too. Lady Randal was charming, but in a very different style from her son. People loved Lady Randal on sight. Her smile was filled with impulsive, spontaneous warmth, and everyone who came into contact with her fell for that smile.

"Lovely, isn't she?" Sir Gee looked at Dinah, beaming from ear to ear.

"Lovely," Dinah agreed, smiling back. Under that busy bouncing manner he was as soft as butter, she thought, especially where his wife was concerned.

"Where was I?" Sir Gee muttered absent-mindedly, running one hand over his bald head. "Oh, yes—Greg. A charmer, like his mother." He shifted uneasily in his chair, and Dinah suddenly realized that he had been planning a little speech. "Don't take him seriously, will you?" His voice was embarrassed. "He's not the marrying kind, though we wish he *would* marry. His mother would love some grandchildren. She wants him to marry her goddaughter—pretty girl, a bit dim, but that's what Maddie wants."

And what his wife wanted Sir Gee was determined she should have, Dinah recognized, catching on at last. Sir Gee would get the moon out of the sky if Lady Randal said she wanted it.

I'm being warned off, she told herself dryly. It was funny. It was hilarious. Sir George had noticed his son flirting with her and was making it clear that Dinah wasn't what Lady Randal wanted for her son. Dinah would have liked to say bluntly that she wouldn't have Greg Randal however much money came with him, but she couldn't do that.

Instead, she said calmly, "I won't take your son seriously, Sir Gee." I wouldn't take your son in any way, shape or form, she thought.

Sir Gee gave a relieved sigh and looked at her

approvingly. "You're a sensible girl, Dinah. I admire you for that."

"Thank you, Sir George," she said in a bland voice before going back to her own office.

She was getting ready to leave that evening when Andrew came into her office, standing in the doorway, hovering, his face anxious.

"Got a minute?"

Dinah smiled at him. "Come in; don't stand there looking as if you're going to bolt at any second."

Andrew Duncan, one of the top executives in the firm, had known Dinah for years. In fact, it had been Andrew who recommended Dinah be promoted to the job with Sir Gee. His family had lived across the street from Dinah's home. She and Andrew had grown up together, since their mothers had been close friends.

He came in and closed the door, leaning against it, his hands stuffed deep in his pockets, studying his feet. Andrew was a very quiet, gentle man with a placid temperament and a great capacity for hard work. He owed his position in the firm to his ability to work well under pressure without getting upset. Even Sir Gee couldn't panic Andrew. He just stood there, foursquare and as solid as a house, facing out the storm which blew every time Sir Gee lost his temper.

Dinah was very fond of him. He was the brother she had never had, and she knew that to Andrew she was the sister he had never had. It was a comfortable relationship. There had never been any romantic feeling between them. They knew each other too well. Andrew had always confided all his love affairs to her,

21

needing some sympathetic ear; and although Dinah was not the type to make confidences in turn, she knew that if ever she did need to talk to someone it would be Andrew she would choose before anyone else.

Now, watching his furrowed brow, she asked gently, "Something wrong, Andy?"

He shrugged his shoulders. "Judy."

Dinah had already guessed it would be, but she said, "What happened this time?"

Andrew had been married to Judy almost a year ago. His wife was a very different type—pretty and lively, but with a moody temperament which had led to frequent rows between her and Andrew. Andrew always rushed to Dinah to get sympathy. He didn't know how to cope with Judy's moods and attitudes. His family background hadn't prepared him to deal with such volatile emotions. His parents were as quiet and calm as Andrew, and in all the years Dinah had known them she had never heard them quarrel.

"She says she wants a divorce," Andrew mumbled, staring at his shoes as though they fascinated him.

"Oh, Andy." Dinah got up and came over to him, taking hold of his wide shoulders in both hands. "Why?"

"Another guy," Andrew said.

"Who?" Although they had been quarreling all year, Dinah had never thought Judy would turn elsewhere. She had assumed Judy's difficult temperament to be at the root of their problems. It hadn't occurred to her that there might be someone else taking Andrew's place in her life.

Andrew shrugged. "She won't say. Says it's none of

my business. She moved out of the flat last night. I don't even know where she's gone or how I can get in touch with her."

"I'm sorry," Dinah said, wishing she knew something she could say to him. He was pale, his face tight with pain. He looked terrible and she could tell he felt even worse.

"I'd no idea," Andrew muttered. "If I knew, I'd beat his brains in. . . ."

Dinah hugged him. "Oh, Andy . . ."

He put his arms around her, holding on tight, burying his face in her shoulder. She could feel him trembling against her and was angry with Judy for doing this to him. How could she? Andrew didn't deserve this. He was much too kind to get this sort of treatment.

Behind them, a door opened suddenly. Andrew straightened, going red, and pushed Dinah away. She spun and found Greg Randal staring at her across the room. Muttering something incoherent, Andrew backed away and fled, slamming the door behind him.

"Sorry to be so inopportune," Greg Randal said, the smile absent from his gray eyes for once. "I was looking for my father."

"He's gone," Dinah stammered, aware that she had flushed. "He left a short time ago."

He nodded, his face expressionless, and went without another word, closing the door behind him with a jerk.

Dinah stood there, frowning. What had he thought as he saw her and Andrew jump apart? She bit her lower lip. She knew what he had thought, of course, but she could hardly run after him and start muttering confused explanations. Let him think what he liked. It was none of his business, and Andrew certainly wouldn't want his private problems broadcast all around the office. What Greg Randal thought was his own problem.

Chapter Two

One morning the following week Dinah's alarm clock failed to go off for the time she had set it. She was awakened by the sound of pneumatic drills instead. Jolting up in bed, she gazed in horror at the time. "Oh, no, I'm going to be late!" She scrambled out of bed and fled to the bathroom, yelling to the two girls who shared the flat as she went, "Late, we're late! The alarm didn't go off on time. Get up!"

They relied on Dinah to get them up. Neither Jennifer nor Dilly liked waking to alarm clocks. They preferred to have Dinah tiptoe in with a cup of tea while she was getting ready. This morning they would have to go without their tea.

There were workmen outside in the road, breaking up the tarmac surface, their drills splitting the air with a horrible noise as Dinah brushed her teeth and rushed to get ready for work.

Jennifer battered on the door. "Hurry up! What are you doing in there?"

Dinah rushed out. "Sorry, the alarm clock didn't go off; I must dash."

"Make some tea," Jennifer moaned as she stumbled into the bathroom, but Dinah called back, "No time, sorry."

Dilly showed no sign of life. Dinah banged on the door as she went past. "Dilly, get up!"

She heard Dilly groan and turn over heavily. Dinah hesitated but really couldn't stop to make sure Dilly got up. She had to get to the office before Sir Gee. Punctuality was a fetish with him. His daily routine mustn't be upset or he would sulk all day. She just *couldn't* be late.

She fought her way down into the underground and caught the tube into the center of London. She was breathless as she emerged from the tin coffin to be carried, crushed and frantic, in the middle of a seething crowd of other office workers out into the city sunlight rushing to start the day's work.

In the lift, on the way up to the top floor, she tried to smooth down her hair, straighten her clothes. She looked as disheveled as she felt. Dinah hated rushing about. She liked to begin her morning in a leisurely way, taking things slowly so everything would be in proper order. It set the pattern for the whole day. Sir Gee was not easy to work for, even on his good days. Dinah had found it helped to start the day in an atmosphere of calm.

When she walked into her office she saw that her worst fears had been realized. Sir Gee was already there; she heard his voice through the door. Picking up the mail, she began to sift through it. Her windows breathed cooling air across the room and she decided to leave them open. Her face was very flushed.

When she was through sorting the mail, Greg Randal was standing by the window, listening to his father. Dinah felt the lance of his cool gray eyes as she offered the letters to Sir Gee.

"You're late," Sir Gee accused, glaring at her.

"I'm sorry; my alarm clock didn't go off."

"I'm never late," Sir Gee muttered.

"You were the day I arrived back," Greg put in without undue emphasis.

"What? Who—me?" Sir Gee's face reddened. "Couple of minutes, that's all. That's not late." He gave Dinah a sulky look. "You're half an hour late."

"I'll make it up this evening," she offered, and he grunted under his breath.

"Forget it, but don't do it again." His eye ran down over the letters. "What's on the diary?"

She told him and he broke in hurriedly, "Can't lunch with him. I've got to go over to St. Mark."

Greg gave a furious exclamation. "Oh, blast! I'd forgotten."

Sir Gee looked at him, bolt-eyed, and bellowed, "Forgotten her birthday, have you? How could you?"

"I'll send her a greetings telegram," Greg offered, his face self-accusing.

"She'll know you forgot, then," gobbled Sir Gee, his face as red as a turkey-cock's. "She's ninety-two, remember. She isn't going to have many more birthdays. You might remember the ones she has. She *is* your grandmother."

The Randal family were a close-knit group and took

all their anniversaries seriously. Sir Gee's mother was a tiny bird of a woman with eyes as sharp as knives and a mind to match them, for all her age. Every birthday was a triumph to her now. Sir Gee was very proud of his mother's great age, but Mrs. Randal was prouder still. She boasted of it to everyone she met, however casual the meeting. Dinah had sometimes been down to the little village of St. Mark with Sir Gee, and as soon as Mrs. Randal set eyes on her she would gleefully ask Dinah how old she thought she was and watch with satisfaction as Dinah expressed amazement.

Greg moved restlessly. "I can't think how it slipped my mind."

"Didn't slip mine." Sir Gee conveniently forgot that it had been Dinah who had reminded him, as she reminded him of everything. "I sent her a card," Sir Gee went on. "Chose it myself."

Out of a box of fifty which Dinah kept in her stationery cupboard, in fact. Sir Gee liked sending birthday cards to people. He did it all the time, often astonishing the recipient. Only last week he had sent one to a member of the steno pool, a newcomer to the staff. Dinah had casually mentioned to Sir Gee that it was Sharon's birthday, and Sir Gee had at once begun sorting through his cards. Sharon had been over-whelmed. "Oh, isn't he a lovely man?" she had said all day.

Greg pushed one of his long, sinewy hands through his hair, ruffling it into untidy peaks. "I'll drive down there," he said. "And I'll make my apologies to her in person." He was obviously fond of his grandmother, although he didn't make such a song and dance about it as Sir Gee did. Dinah had already realized that Greg

Randal didn't carry his heart on his sleeve. She had seen him with his mother the other day and realized that Greg definitely felt as strongly about Lady Randal as his father did, but he was far less obvious about it.

He puzzled Dinah, in fact. Her initial impression of him had given way to other feelings over the past week. He had been in and out of the office all the time, but his teasing charm had not been so much in evidence. She had seen him brisk and businesslike as he began to take over his department. He might not resemble his father visually, but Dinah could already see that Greg Randal was going to be a pretty tough customer to handle in the office.

"Can't come to lunch," Sir Gee told him. "You'll have to take my lunch date with Sir Lawrence."

"Why don't I drive down after that?" Greg suggested.

"Mrs. Watson won't like it," Sir Gee said. "You know she hates unexpected guests."

"Tell her I'm coming, then," Greg retorted.

Sir Gee looked sulky. "Why don't you tell her yourself." He was terrified of his mother's house-keeper-companion, a formidable lady who either wore whalebone corsets or had an extraordinary figure. Her iron-gray hair, piercing eyes and deep voice made her daunting, but although she terrorized Sir Gee with a look, Dinah was convinced Mrs. Watson had a weakness for him which she only just hid. Whenever he went down to St. Mark, Mrs. Watson always made sure his favorite meals were served.

Greg moved over to pick up the phone. Dinah moved back too late. As he leaned over the desk his long thigh touched her and she shifted uneasily, getting an oblique mocking look from him as he noted her reaction.

He made her feel far too self-conscious. She resented being so aware of him. And she wondered if he realized. Dinah didn't want to react when he came close or ran those speculative eyes over her.

"Mrs. Watson? Greg here," he said, and Dinah moved away to check Sir Gee's out tray, trying not to listen as Greg talked. He had a voice like honey, she thought, warm and melting. The other day she had heard him talking to one of the outer-office girls like that. He had quite a technique. It worked like a charm with the girls out there, but Dinah found it set her teeth on edge. She had to force herself to smile when one of the girls began raving about how fantastic he was, what charm, what looks, what a wonderful voice. Couldn't they see through him?

As Greg put the phone down Sir Gee said gleefully, "Nasty, was she?"

"A bit grim," Greg agreed. "I had to work hard to coax a kind word out of her. Grandmother's livid with me."

"Can't blame her." Sir Gee nodded. "You shouldn't have forgotten. You've only got one grandparent."

"I could kick myself," Greg muttered.

"I'll do it for you," his father offered, laughing. He looked at Dinah. "Like to join me, Dinah?"

She smiled coldly. Greg swung around to eye her as though daring her to agree.

"Dinah will fill you in on the details of the Paris negotiations," Sir Gee went on, returning to business. "Larry has been haggling over a price for months— Dinah has all the documents. Nail him down today, the slippery old eel. I want it cut and dried. He's dragging things out, and I'm sick of it."

Greg took his usual seat on the edge of his father's desk. "I'd better have a look at the file. I'm not sure of the details."

"Where is it?" Sir Gee asked Dinah, and she flicked through her memory.

"You took it home with you the other day."

Sir Gee looked shifty. "I left it there," he admitted. "Oh, blast. I knew there was something I should have remembered."

"Shall I send a car for it?"

Sir Gee hesitated, then shook his head. "I've got a better idea. You go along with Greg. You know it all by heart. Fill him in on the details before lunch."

Greg moved to the door. "That's settled," he said as he left, and Dinah glared after him.

"I've got a lunch date," she told Sir Gee indignantly, and he gave her a coaxing little smile.

"Sorry, Dinah, but we have to keep Greg happy."

"He has too many people doing that already," Dinah muttered as she went out. In her own office she sat with a scowl, staring at the phone. She did not want to break her date, certainly not to sit through a tedious business lunch with Greg Randal and Sir Lawrence Smith, a man she detested. With a sigh, she picked up the phone and dialed.

Mark's secretary answered. "He's out on site," she told Dinah offhandedly.

Mark Carew was one of the architects who worked for the organization. His firm had designed the complex, although it had been Mark's senior partner who had been responsible for the winning design.

Mark was a tall, long-limbed man with rough brown hair, a rugged, weathered face and a calm manner which she found to be soothing. They had discovered mutual tastes on their first meeting. It wasn't often that you discovered someone who shared your own very individual passion for things like radio soap opera and old silent movies. They had met one night at a party and talked together all evening long without noticing anyone else around them.

The relationship was still new, though. A second date was a tricky thing. At such an early stage one was always uncertain, wondering if the other person really wanted to see you again, and Mark might think she had stood him up because she couldn't be bothered to meet him for lunch this afternoon. It was a pity he wasn't in the office, Dinah thought grimly as she left a message. It would have been easier to make it clear that she would have loved to keep their date, but business was what was keeping her from meeting him.

She thought of Greg Randal with disfavor. It had never even entered his head to ask if she minded joining him for lunch. Her convenience wasn't something that bothered him.

Dinah picked her men with care. She wasn't the type of girl to rush into anything, especially a relationship with a man. She viewed the world coolly from a distance, her temperament inclining her to be wary. The only time she had fallen in love at first sight she had ended up with a broken heart. And she surely didn't want that to ever happen again. She had learned at eighteen that it was a mistake to rush into things. She refused to lose her cool over any man, but she particularly disliked men who tried to rush her. She didn't trust men with charm, men who flirted lightly. Mark was the sort of man you could trust. He never flirted, and he didn't rush anything. He took his time and let things take their own course, without pushing. He was an intelligent, levelheaded man with a quiet sense of humor, and she hoped he would not be offended that she had broken their lunch date.

At noon Greg Randal strolled into her office, elegant in a dark, formal suit which he somehow managed to make sexy despite its sober tailoring. It was the way he wore it, Dinah decided, eyeing him through her lashes while she went on with her work. The cut and style might be conservative and restrained, but that lean-hipped body conveyed a very different feeling.

"Ready?" he asked when she gave no hint of stopping work.

Dinah rolled the paper out of her typewriter and nodded, getting up.

"My father tells me you had to break a date," he murmured, watching her. "Sorry."

He hardly sounded it, Dinah thought rebelliously.

"I hope he wasn't annoyed," Greg said, his voice as smooth as cream.

He was fishing, she realized, and she didn't even bother to answer. She had no intention of telling Greg Randal about her private life. It was none of his business.

"You've got a mind like a locked safe," he muttered after a pause.

Dinah ignored that. As they went down in the lift she went through all the details she remembered of the negotiations with Sir Lawrence Smith's company. The organization was buying a large office block in Paris from him. They were expanding into France, and it was a matter of urgency for them to get that building.

"Your memory is phenomenal," he congratulated her when she had finished.

They were just entering the hotel where they were to meet Sir Lawrence later. Dinah absently noticed that Greg Randal's skin had a smooth brown gleam in the London sunlight. He had recently been to Florida, she remembered. Nice for him, she thought. I wish I could fly off to Florida.

A small party of Japanese rushed out, almost knocking Dinah over, and Greg's hand slid under her elbow to draw her aside. She quickly disengaged herself and got a sideways look from him.

"I don't exactly turn you on, do I?" he asked dryly.

She looked at her watch. "We're early."

"Don't you ever answer questions?"

"Why should I?" She met his eyes directly.

"Why shouldn't you?"

"You ask the wrong questions."

"Tell me the right ones," he suggested.

"Mr. Randal, I work for your father. Ask me anything about my job and I'll be only too happy to answer. My private life and my personal opinions are my own business."

"You do have a private life, then," he commented, striding beside her through the great echoing marble lobby of the hotel.

"Who doesn't?" Dinah insinctively made her way toward the bar. Whenever she lunched here with Sir Gee he always had a drink there first.

"I wondered," Greg murmured, sinking down beside her on the deep leather couch she chose.

Dinah looked down her nose. "Carry on wondering." The waiter hovered in front of them, and Greg lifted an eyebrow to ask what she wanted to drink.

"White wine, please."

When the waiter had gone Greg shifted and Dinah's skin prickled. He was sitting far too close. It oppressed her to feel that long, lean body lounging beside her.

"What have you got against me?" he asked plaintively. "Every time I come into the office I get an icy reception."

He couldn't bear it because she wasn't one of his throng of admirers, Dinah realized. You met them in both sexes—the sort of people who have to knock out everyone they meet at first sight. If they fail to do so it drives them totally mad.

In Sir Gee that determination to win was expressed in his sales techniques. He kept on pushing his product until it finally sold because the public had been browbeaten into wanting it. Greg used the same psychology with women, she imagined. Dinah shifted away from him. He could cross her off his list. She wasn't a buying market where he was concerned.

"Is Andrew Duncan your private life?"

The terse question stunned her. A flush crept over her face and her blue eyes shot to him before she had had time to mask her immediate reaction to his probing question.

Greg was watching her like a hawk, his gray eyes iced over. "He's married, isn't he?" he demanded.

Dinah moistened her lips, her face nervously angry.

35

"I'm not going to discuss Andrew with you, Mr. Randal."

"He's always in your office. You see a lot of each other."

Dinah frowned. "Aren't you observant?" Her tone had a sarcastic ring, and Greg's eyes flashed.

"I've heard he got married only last year."

The waiter arrived with their drinks, and Dinah picked up her glass and sipped it, her face averted, the cool profile tense with annoyance. Why did he think she should confide information about her private life to him? She wasn't plunging into any explanations. It was none of his business.

"Haven't you any compunction about breaking up a marriage that recent?"

"You have no idea what you're talking about," Dinah broke out huskily.

"I know what I saw when I walked in so inconveniently the other day."

"You're jumping to conclusions," she said coldly.

"Obvious ones," he muttered.

"It's always a mistake to accept the obvious," Dinah told him.

Greg began to speak, his voice harsh, but before he had got out more than the first word Sir Lawrence arrived and Greg had to break off to rise and shake hands.

Dinah's relief made her almost sick. She did not enjoy being seen as the other woman in a triangle. Her personal ideals would never have allowed her to accept such a role and she resented having it assumed that she would.

Sir Lawrence was a bland man in his late fifties with a

permanent smile and a mind like a razor. He and Sir Gee had had a running battle ever since they were at school together, each always trying to get the better of the other.

"Marvelous to have you back, Greg," he flattered as he smiled at Greg over the lunch table later, but that smile hid a cold mind which was bent on sizing Greg up and somehow running rings around him.

Dinah wasn't fooled by all those phony smiles. She sat back to watch the polite and deadly duel, wondering which of these two gentlemen would emerge as the victor.

Today Greg had a restless impatience which reminded her of his father. He might be treating Sir Lawrence with kid gloves, but Greg was determined to end the deadlock over the negotiations.

"I'm afraid we're not going to raise the offer, you know," he told Sir Lawrence. "If we could, we would, but it's out of the question. That's our final offer."

"You wouldn't find anywhere more suitable in the whole of Paris," Sir Lawrence assured him.

Greg shrugged. "You may be right, but at that price we would have to back off and take whatever we could get at a lower figure."

Sir Lawrence showed his teeth in what only just passed for a smile. "That would be shortsighted, surely?"

"Needs must when the devil drives." Greg sighed, turning to the waiter. "We'll have liqueurs with our coffee. Dinah, what will you have?"

"Cointreau," she said.

The two men had large snifters of brandy which they used as props, swirling the amber liquid around as they argued with a smiling blandness which did not disguise the tough bargaining which was really going on beneath those smiles. It seemed like a game to Dinah.

Dinah let the orange zest of the smooth liqueur linger on her tongue, listening intently to what the two men had to say. Now and then Greg turned to ask her some question about the past negotiations, drawing her into the duel to back him up.

The end came suddenly. Sir Lawrence gave a long sigh and held out his hand. "What can't be cured must be endured."

Greg grinned. "You won a good price from us, and you know it."

"My dear boy, you held your own, and *you* know it. You take after your father."

"I'll accept that as a compliment," Greg told him smoothly.

Sir Lawrence gave him a dry look. "Let's say I meant it as one. I wish I had a son like you." He had three daughters but no sons and it was an open secret that he disliked all his girls.

Glancing at his watch, Sir Lawrence rose. "I must be off, I'm afraid. I'll have to break it to my board that we must accept your price."

"Break it gently," Greg said, amused.

Sir Lawrence smiled back before he left, and Greg called the waiter over. "Another liqueur, Dinah?" He was delighted with his success, she realized, but she refused. She couldn't work this afternoon if she drank more than a little at lunch. It made her head much too cloudy for details.

"We pulled it off," Greg said, and Dinah shook her head.

"We? I didn't do a thing, just sat and listened."

"Ah, but he knew you were there," Greg pointed out. "And he knew he couldn't try any sleight of hand on me about those figures with you listening. Your amazing memory for detail is famous."

Flattering, Dinah thought, but how much of it does he mean? That was the trouble with a man like Greg Randal. His smile, his charm, made her cautious about believing a word he said.

On their way back to the office Greg was quiet, staring out the window, and she was relieved about that because she had had a nervous suspicion that he might return to the subject of Andrew Duncan and what part he played in her life.

Greg vanished as soon as they had entered the office block. Dinah went back to work, grateful that Sir Gee's absence gave her a chance to catch up on some of the neglected filing that had begun to pile up.

She was able to finish it all before Sir Gee erupted into the office at five o'clock. "Come through, come through," he bellowed from the door. "Got to get on—running behind time."

Dinah went through the phone messages and telex communications from the various offices across the world, got him to sign his letters and began to give him a report on the lunch with Sir Lawrence Smith and Greg. In the middle of her rapid breakdown of what had happened, Greg arrived. His father slapped him on the back.

"Well done."

Greg laughed. "You've heard?"

39

"Dinah was just telling me what a wonderful job you did."

Dinah moved off to her own office, leaving them talking, but just as she was about to leave Andrew joined her, a harassed expression on his face.

She looked at him with distress. "More trouble?" Judy had not been in touch with him at all since she left their flat, but, through her parents, Andrew had learned that she was living in a small flat on her own somewhere. He had been trying to get in touch with her, but she was ignoring all the letters he sent to her family home to be forwarded to her.

He sighed. "Only the same thing."

"Can't you persuade her parents to intervene?"

"They're being very offhand," Andrew said disconsolately. "I get the feeling they blame me, although heaven knows I've leaned over backward to make her happy."

Perhaps that was the trouble, Dinah thought. Andrew was always too eager to compromise, to give in to Judy's volatile moods. Maybe he ought to have been more forceful with her instead of letting her have her way all the time. Judy kept pushing him and Andrew kept giving way. Dinah wouldn't enjoy a marriage built on such a relationship. It would have made her feel that her husband was only humoring her, and that wasn't any basis for a good marriage.

"You haven't a clue who the other man is yet?" She knew that Andrew had been spending hours trying to talk Judy's parents into telling him exactly what was going on between Judy and this other man. And exactly who this other man was.

He scowled. "Not a shred of an idea. It has to be

someone she works with, I reckon. She never met anyone else, unless she met him casually, and Judy isn't the type to let herself be picked up by strangers." His wide shoulders sagged. "Or is she? How would I know? I'm beginning to think I don't know her at all. I don't think I ever knew her." His mouth had a miserable curve to it. "Women baffle me. I can't make head nor tail of their thinkings or doings."

Dinah watched him with a wry expression. "Poor Andy." He was right, though. He was far from an expert on the subject. Andrew had never been able to manage his relationships with girls. He had always flown to Dinah to ask her advice, to plead for enlightenment when some girl proved difficult. Andrew just didn't understand the opposite sex, however hard he tried.

"Why don't we have dinner and talk about it?" he asked her eagerly. "I'm sick of spending my evenings alone in front of the TV."

"I'd love to," she said easily.

"Great. I knew I could count on you, Dinah," he said gratefully.

They left the building together. The receptionist gave them one of her blank, mechanical smiles as they passed. "Good night."

"Good night," Dinah said, wondering if she went home or was just switched off by the night watchman when everyone else had gone. A sudden summer shower had begun, and they had to dash down to the car park which took up the basement of the building. While Andrew unlocked his car Dinah leaned on the bonnet, idly watching another car as it appeared from the far end of the car park.

It slowed as it passed, and Dinah felt her nerves prickle as she met Greg Randal's gray glance. He shot a look at Andrew and then looked back at her, his lip curling. And what seemed to be an arrogant, knowing look gleamed in his eyes.

A second later he had gone, his exhaust leaving a fine trail of smoke in the quiet air.

"Something wrong?" Andrew asked as he joined her in the car a moment later and noticed her frown.

Pulling herself together, Dinah shook her head. "Not a thing," she said.

"You look grim."

"Nothing important," Dinah assured him. Why should she care if Greg Randal looked at her with contempt?

Chapter Three

She told herself the same thing a number of times over the following weeks. Greg was in and out of her office all the time, but whenever they met he gave her a blank stare, as though he had difficulty remembering who she was, or preferred to forget. Dinah found she did not like that look he kept giving her. She knew what was behind it, and it made her feel both angry and unhappy. It wasn't pleasant being despised, especially when you knew it was undeserved, but she wasn't going to put him right. He shouldn't make judgments on such small evidence. And just how was it his concern anyway? She worked for his father, and no matter what she did with her personal life, it was really no business of his. Why was he reacting so?

And her personal life wasn't what she wanted it to be either. She had several dates with Mark, but somehow their relationship had never recovered from that canceled lunch. Mark withdrew without being obvious about it. That annoyed Dinah, too. She was not the sort of girl who could blatantly angle for dates. She tried to make it clear that she liked Mark and enjoyed his company, but she could tell that Mark was treating her warily.

"My personal life is a mess," she told Jennifer with a groan.

Her flatmate looked up from the paperback she was reading. "So what's new? Whose isn't?"

"Yours seems to be fine."

"Today it is—tomorrow it could be a disaster area." Jennifer had a glamorous job in a London fashion house as an assistant buyer and had met some fascinating men. She flew in and out of love like a homing pigeon; but she wasn't in a hurry to settle down, and a bad case of love only bothered her for a few weeks. She recovered from it unscathed and was off again with the next good-looking male who hove into view.

Dinah envied her that cheerful adaptability. They had been at school together for years. It was one of those friendships which have no basis in mutual tastes or characters, yet exist for years by some freak of coincidence. They had just happened to get jobs in the same exclusive area of London after leaving school, and used to bump into each other in the street now and then, exchanging news and small talk. Discovering that they were both flat-hunting at the same time, they had joined forces. It was easier to get a flat in London if you had someone ready to share it. It was also a lot less expensive.

Dinah had had doubts about sharing a flat with

Jennifer, but, as it turned out, it had worked out extremely well. They saw very little of each other. Jennifer led a very active social life, but she was an even-tempered girl and they never argued. Sharing a flat was only possible if you compromised. And she and Jennifer got along fine.

"I thought you were keen on this Mark," Jennifer asked, keeping a finger in her book.

Dinah sighed. "I was—he was nice."

"Oh, well, more fish in the sea," Jennifer soothed, shrugging.

"For you, maybe," Dinah said wryly.

Suddenly the front door of the flat flew open and a girl rushed into the living room, sped across it without looking at them and dived into the bathroom, slamming the door behind her.

Jennifer and Dinah looked at each other. "Not again," Jennifer groaned.

They listened for sounds of movement and heard the bath taps running. "She could just be having a bath," Dinah suggested.

"Drowning herself in it," Jennifer muttered. "I forgot to tell you—she had a letter from Hamish this morning. He's gone to Aberdeen with a girl he met at a party."

"Oh, no," Dinah said. Hamish was always doing it. Whenever he got fed up with London he was off over the border, home to Scotland, swearing never to return.

"I want to get into the bathroom in half an hour," Jennifer complained. "My black tights are drying over the radiator."

"Ask her to pass them through the door."

"You know she won't open up once she's gone to ground."

Dinah knew only too well. Every time Dilly had one of these crisis points she shut herself into the bathroom and refused to come out. Dilly met life like a surfer with a death wish. She flung herself violently into anguish of mind at the drop of a hat.

Listening at the bathroom door, she heard sobbing. "Dilly, darling," she cooed softly.

Howl, went Dilly. It was the only answer Dinah got. She crouched down to peer through the keyhole and got a distorted view of the bath with Dilly's bright orange head bobbing about in it. Was she getting ready to drown herself or just replacing the tears she had already shed?

That's all the hot water gone, Dinah thought. She had been planning on a bath herself. She was worn to a frazzle after a very tough day. Sir Gee had been bouncing about like a rubber ball since nine o'clock that morning, with Dinah hurrying after him everywhere he went. He had bounced off at six, as lively as ever, but Dinah felt like a walking corpse. For a man of his age he had more energy than was good for those around him.

"Dilly, will you be long?" She tried to sound calm and relaxed because sometimes it made Dilly respond.

Today she only got silence in reply.

"Jennifer wants to have a bath, too," Dinah pointed out. "Don't be selfish, Dilly. If you stay in that bath all evening, you'll shrink."

Dilly ignored her, the pink, tear-stained face just visible through the cloud of steam.

"What are we going to do about her?" Jennifer asked with a sigh.

Dinah shrugged. "Who knows anymore?"

On sight they both had been doubtful about Dilly's suitability as a flatmate. She had arrived to meet them in baggy pants and a red check shirt, looking like a disheveled clown. There had been several girls wanting to share the flat with them, and all of them had been more suitable than Dilly. Yet somehow it had been Dilly who had moved in with them a few weeks later. Neither Jennifer nor Dinah was sure why, but they had offered her the third bedroom on a crazy impulse which they had alternately regretted and rejoiced in ever since.

Dilly was untidy, impulsive and emotional. She was a health-food freak and left half-eaten yogurt everywhere. She wore appalling clothes and played rock music at a volume which made you feel you were having it nailed through your head. She drove them up the wall, and they worried themselves silly about her.

"It's time she grew up," Dinah muttered. Dilly admitted to twenty, but from her behavior she was probably younger. They should never have let her move into the flat. Her lifestyle just didn't match theirs. Yet having once let Dilly into their lives they found it impossible to kick her out again. It would be like evicting a stray kitten. And besides, they did truly care about her.

Jennifer shrugged. "I've got to get ready. My date will be calling for me any time now." She went off to her own room, and Dinah considered the problem of Dilly with a frown.

"For heaven's sake, do come out, Dilly," she implored without success.

The doorbell went and Jennifer yelled, "Get it and ask him to hang on for a minute, will you?"

Dinah opened the front door, a polite smile ready. Her blue eyes opened wide. "Oh, it's you." Surprise made her voice rise.

"Yes," agreed Greg Randal. "It's me. Sorry to trouble you at home, but my father lost the speech he's supposed to be giving to that group of Italian businessmen."

She had never seen him in jeans and a sweater before. In the office he habitually wore those elegant dark suits and formal striped shirts, his hair always brushed down. Tonight it was tossed into windswept black disorder. He looked totally different, and Dinah was silenced for a moment by this new impression of him.

His brows rose in sardonic response to her openmouthed astonishment. "Have you got it?"

"What?" She hadn't really heard his first question. She had been too absorbed in staring at him.

"The speech," he prompted.

"Oh," Dinah said, moving back. "Come in . . . I'll take a look through my things." She had picked up a great wad of documents to bring home with her. Part of her job entailed reading over reports from the far-flung outposts of the Randal empire, and she never seemed to get time to do it in the office, with Sir Gee around. Dinah often brought stuff home to work on in her spare time.

He walked into the living room and stared around him in open curiosity. "So this is where you live."

It was crowded, shabby and untidy, but Dinah wasn't about to apologize for her home. She went over to pick up the heap of papers she had dumped on the table earlier, flicking through them in search of Sir Gee's speech.

"Do you live here alone?" Greg asked in a strange, terse voice. Dinah turned and saw him staring at a little pile of ironed men's shirts which Dilly had left there that morning. Heaven alone knew how long they would sit waiting for his return. Dilly did all Hamish's washing and ironing for him. She tidied his flat, too. Dilly was a born slave. Dinah and Jennifer had urged her over and over again not to turn herself into a doormat for Hamish to walk all over, but Dilly blithely went on doing it.

"No," Dinah said, equally terse. It didn't need two guesses to see what was in his mind, and she resented the assumption.

He didn't answer, staring at the shirts with his black brows drawn in a heavy line across his forehead.

The bathroom door jerked open. Draped in an enormous white towel and looking like a tragic Roman, Dilly stalked out with her nose in the air. Only when she was actually in the room did she notice Greg, and then, giving him a horrified look, she bolted, clutching her towel around her.

Greg stared after her before turning to look at Dinah. "Who was that in the toga?"

"One of my flatmates," Dinah said tartly.

"How many of them are there?" He had relaxed and was smiling slightly. "She looked about twelve."

"I often think she is," Dinah muttered, still search-

49

ing through the documents but with her mind not on what she was doing.

Jennifer flew into the room, glossy from head to toe in a smooth coffee-colored dress which clung to every inch of her. She had her party smile ready. It withered as she saw Greg.

"Oh," she said.

Greg rose. "Hello," he murmured with unhidden interest.

Jennifer smiled. It was the smile she gave men she found worth a second look.

Dinah had found Sir Gee's speech. She pulled it out and turned toward Greg with it. The sooner he left, the better, as far as she was concerned.

Jennifer was talking to him, posing with a hand on one hip in one of her favorite model angles. "Like some coffee?" she asked, and Greg, to Dinah's fury, said he would love some.

"Hadn't you better get back to your father with this?" Dinah asked, offering him the speech and hoping he'd leave.

He took the immaculately typed sheets and stuffed them under his arm in what she considered to be a highly casual manner. "Plenty of time; he isn't on his feet until nine."

Jennifer sank into a corner of the couch with elegant movements. "Make some coffee, Di."

Dinah's lips folded into a tight line, but she withdrew to the kitchen. Jennifer had a nerve, she thought, angrily plugging in the electric kettle. How was she going to explain Greg's presence to her date when he arrived? Getting down some of the bright orange

50

earthenware mugs, she listened to the sound of Greg Randal laughing and the murmur of his deep voice, and found nothing enjoyable in either.

Jennifer fancied him, she told herself dryly. Nothing surprising in that, of course. So did most of the female staff in the Randal offices. He had been through them like the common cold, striking them down one by one with unerring accuracy, but by some magical technique of his own remaining on lighthearted terms with his victims. His arrival in an office was the signal for an outbreak of smiles. He didn't get many from Dinah, though, nor did she get many from him. Whenever they met they looked at each other distantly and were horribly polite to each other.

It got a bit wearing. Dinah did not like having someone treat her like an infectious disease.

Dilly flew into the kitchen, her face flushed. The towel had gone and was replaced by figure-hugging black jeans and a daringly skimpy white top. Her mop of orange hair had been ruthlessly brushed into curls and her brown eyes were dilated with excitement. Oh, no, thought Dinah, not Dilly, too?

"Who is *he?*" Dilly demanded excitedly. "Wow, he's fantastic."

"Join the club," Dinah said wearily. "You can take him his coffee."

"Can I?" Dilly accepted the proffered mug with an expression of reverence and tiptoed off with it like someone on her way to a shrine.

Dinah took the tray and loaded it with three other mugs. Just as she appeared in the living room Jennifer's date arrived. With a glum face Jennifer departed with him, throwing Greg a last wistful smile over her shoulder.

Dilly took Jennifer's vacated place beside him quickly, fluttering her eyelashes. "I'm Belinda," she said. She only used her real name when she wanted to impress people. Dinah saw her secretly measuring herself against Greg's impressive height. Dilly adored tall men, she often told them, which seemed a surprising statement from a girl who had been madly in love for years with a short, slight Scot. Hamish was more or less the same height as Dilly, and very skinny, his sharp-featured face belligerent even when he wasn't in a rage. Although he was small, he was famous for his temper. Dilly said that men twice his height backed off when Hamish got mad.

"What do you do?" Greg asked Dilly, who began to tell him about her job in a Chelsea boutique. It was tiny and badly lit. Dilly often didn't show up for work, and the proprietor rarely seemed to notice because the shop was so dark it was hard to tell if anyone was in it or not.

"Shouldn't you get off with that script?" Dinah suggested politely after ten minutes.

Dilly went pink. She wasn't a girl pink suited—it shrieked at her hair. Giving Dinah a furious look, she curled up closer to Greg. "You don't have to go yet, do you?"

He eyed her with amused appreciation. There was something very appealing about Dilly. Men found her reckless vulnerability rather endearing. "Why not come along?" he asked. "I'll deliver this speech to my father; then we'll go have a drink together somewhere special."

Dilly glowed. "I'd love to."

Flicking his eyes to Dinah, Greg asked, "What about you?"

Dilly's mouth turned down at the corners. Dinah observed it with wry displeasure. "Thanks, but I'm expecting someone," she said. It was a lie, but it got her out of a difficult situation.

Greg's face went blank, but Dilly said innocently, and with unhidden pleasure, "Andrew coming around to see you?"

Dinah met her eyes. "Anything can happen," she said dryly, and Dilly looked sheepish.

Greg stood up abruptly, his long limbs uncoiling in a sharp movement. "Ready?" he asked Dilly as he turned toward the door.

"Yes," she said breathlessly, scurrying after him. The front door slammed behind them.

Dinah collected the coffee mugs in an automatic way, frowning. She hoped Dilly knew what she was doing. Greg Randal was way out of her league. Dilly was hardly the sophisticated type he was used to, after all. And Dinah didn't want to see Dilly hurt.

Greg Randal was a very different type from his father. Sir Gee had a live-wire energy which carried him through the toughest schedules, but he was somehow lovable, a man with high animal spirits and an occasional burst of sheer sentimentality which, however, never broke through into his business life. He had a passion for dogs and kept three of them. He chose to claim he only liked them because it was good exercise to take them for a daily walk, but secretly he adored them all.

Greg's favorite exercise, Dinah suspected, had nothing to do with keeping fit, and his pets were human, not animal. His energy was as vital as his father's, but he was more controlled in his use of it. He didn't exert himself unless he chose to do so, but when he saw fit he could make sparks fly.

Office gossip had already been busy coupling his name with those of a number of very pretty ladies. Greg Randal believed in safety in numbers. He was rarely seen with the same girl twice. Dinah could understand why Sir Gee had said he wasn't the marrying kind. She must warn Dilly when she got her alone, she told herself, but she wasn't very optimistic about the outcome. She and Jennifer had talked themselves hoarse warning Dilly about Hamish, and it had done absolutely no good. So why should she listen this time? Dilly wasn't merely a girl with a slave mentality, she was obstinate about it.

Over the next couple of days she had no chance to talk to Dilly about anything. She was too busy herself, and Dilly never seemed to be in the flat when Dinah was there.

"What *is* she up to?" Dinah asked Jennifer over a late-night cup of cocoa.

Jennifer shrugged. "It isn't Hamish, I know that."

Dinah sighed. I hope it isn't Greg Randal, she thought. That could be worse. Dinah had a sinking suspicion that Greg Randal could be even more habit-forming.

Mark came into the office the next morning. He had an appointment with Sir Gee and was early, deliberately. Dinah was very busy when he walked into the office, her face distracted. "Oh, hi," she said, looking up with a start.

Mark smiled at her gravely. "How are you? I haven't seen much of you lately, have I?"

"No," she agreed, half her mind on the tape she was typing from. She switched off the audio machine and turned her attention to Mark.

"Doing anything tonight?" he asked. "Why don't we have dinner?"

Dinah meant to accept. The words were on the tip of her tongue. Yet she didn't say them. Instead, she smiled and shook her head. "I'd have loved to, but I'm very busy."

Now why did I say that? she asked herself as Mark straightened, faintly red. "Oh, well," he muttered. "Some other time, maybe."

He wouldn't ask again. Dinah could tell that. She could have kicked herself. Yet when it came to the point she just hadn't wanted to go out with him, which was ridiculous, because he was a very nice man and she had enjoyed his company.

When he had gone she stared out of the window, asking herself why she had turned him down. The only reason she could come up with was that it hadn't seemed to matter whether she saw him or not. It was hardly a deathless romance. Mark was nice, but . . . There was a lot of ground in that tiny word. It meant nothing, yet it meant everything.

Dinah had never told herself that she was waiting for the one life-or-death love affair. She had always been so sure that marriage was a matter of compatibility, shared tastes, shared attitudes. She wasn't hooked on the idea of intense passion. The idea made her feel rather alarmed, in fact. Yet, although Mark seemed exactly the sort of man she wanted, there had been something missing. Some essential spark had failed to materialize between them. Mark was as exciting as a glass of milk. That special feeling that Dinah felt should be there just wasn't.

It was a very hot afternoon. The great windows of the surrounding office blocks glittered with reflected sunshine, and Dinah found it hard to concentrate, her eye continually drawn to the beautiful blue sky above. She thought with yearning of a beach: foam-topped waves creaming up on the sands and nothing to do but relax in the shade of a sun umbrella and enjoy the warm, lovely day.

When the telephone rang she started in surprise, groping for the receiver and saying vaguely, "Hello?"

"Greg Randal here." He hadn't needed to tell her that. She had recognized his deep tones at the first syllable. "I'm down at my grandmother's house. She has had a slight stroke."

"Oh, no," Dinah interrupted in dismay. She was fond of Sir Gee's mother. "How is she?"

"Her doctor tells me she'll do," Greg said dryly. "It was more of a warning than a serious stroke. She had been gardening, would you believe? In blazing sunshine, too."

Dinah laughed, her face relaxing in relief. "She's amazing, isn't she?" She had a vision of Mrs. Randal trotting about her garden, ignoring her housekeeper's dire warnings.

"She's pigheaded," Greg said. "Let's hope she takes some notice of what her doctor has been telling her about taking things easy. She's got to slow down. At ninety-two she should be more careful." He paused. "I think my father should come down here, though. Can you get hold of him?"

"He's in a board meeting," Dinah told him. "I'll speak to him right away."

The paneled boardroom was crowded with men in shirt sleeves, their jackets discarded in the heat, ties opened loosely at their necks. Sir Gee sat at the head of the table, listening with a glowering expression to one of them, his fingers tapping the table in front of him in a way which boded no good for the perspiring executive. When Sir Gee did not agree with someone he made no bones about letting them know.

Dinah tiptoed around the table, some of the men eyeing her with smiling curiosity, and whispered in Sir Gee's ear as he turned with a scowl to look at her.

"Oh, no!" he burst out, leaping up. The papers in front of him scattered all over the floor, and some of the executives rushed to gather them up. Sir Gee ignored them, staring at Dinah with anxious eyes. "How is she? Bad, was it?"

"No," Dinah soothed gently. "They think you should go down to see her at once, though."

Forgetting the waiting board of directors, Sir Gee rolled off toward the door, remembered them and stopped to give them a cursory glance. "My mother," he said. "Had a stroke. Got to go."

There was a murmur of sympathy, which he ignored as he rushed off, and the board dissolved in his wake, collecting the papers they had been working on and stuffing them into briefcases. One or two of the men began to question Dinah, who parried their curiosity before she followed Sir Gee to his office.

He was on the point of leaving with his briefcase

under his arm. "What did Greg say?" he demanded as she appeared. "How did it happen?"

"She was gardening," Dinah began, and he gave a yelp of rage.

"I've warned her. She never listens to me. I don't like it. I won't have it. Gardening—at her age!"

Dinah looked at him rather anxiously. His round face highly flushed, he looked as if he might be going to have a stroke himself.

"Has my wife been told?"

Dinah told him she didn't know. "Better give her a ring," Sir Gee commanded. He paused. "No, I'll do it. Get my home, will you?" He chewed on his full lower lip. "Don't want Maddie upset."

Lady Randal already knew, Dinah discovered, and was on her way to see her mother-in-law right now. Sir Gee barely waited to hear that before he was on his way to the door. Concerned, Dinah followed him, and he halted to say, "Come with me, Dinah." It was a mumbled appeal rather than an order. She saw that Sir Gee was deeply alarmed, very anxious. His family was the most important thing in his life, far outweighing the business empire he ran with such energy and efficiency. Grabbing up her own possessions, Dinah followed him to the lift.

On the drive he kept erupting with angry worry. "Women are the devil. Never listen to a word you say. Does she think she's immortal?"

Probably, Dinah thought, half smiling. Mrs. Randal had always struck her as having the same obstinate determination as her son.

When they reached the pleasant country house set on

the edge of a little Kent village, it was Lady Randal
who met her husband at the door. She gave him a
warm, reassuring smile. "She's doing very well." Lady
Randal knew her husband's devotion to his mother.

He sagged. "Sure?"

He's like a child, Dinah thought, watching the calm
way his wife led him into the house.

He charged off up the stairs, and Lady Randal turned
to greet Dinah. "How are you?" she asked. "I haven't
seen you to talk to for ages. Come and have some tea.
You probably need it if you've had to listen to Gee all
the way from London."

"He was desperately worried," Dinah murmured,
and his wife smiled lovingly.

"I'm sure he was; he adores her, you know. Gee
wouldn't know what to do with himself if anything
happened to her. He hates to have changes in his life.
Men do, haven't you noticed that? They're conservative by nature. They like the same people around them,
the same routine every day." Lady Randal gestured to
an armchair. "Sugar? Milk?"

Dinah replied and accepted the cup, her glance
moving over the comfortable sitting room. It was
furnished in a timeless English way with silk brocades
and walnut furniture, the faint air of age which lay on
everything only increasing the charm of the impression.

Greg came into the room a few moments later and
told his mother that Sir Gee was creating havoc upstairs. "Oh, dear," Lady Randal said, getting up without undue anxiety. "What's he up to now?"

"Quarreling with Grandmother over her gardening,"
said Greg. "They're at it hammer and tongs."

Lady Randal sighed and went out, and Greg sank into a chair facing Dinah. "Tea? I need a cup," he said, leaning forward to pour himself one.

A distant crash of thunder signaled the arrival of a summer storm. The room darkened abruptly and then flashed with lightning. Dinah jumped, her eyes flying to the window.

"I thought that was coming," Greg told her.

Dinah felt a peculiar nervous flicker running through her body. She stared at the sky, watching the way it split with lightning, the livid clouds jaggedly illuminated by it. She could hear Greg Randal breathing very close to her. He shifted in his chair, and she felt the movement as though he had touched her, her eyes turning toward him with a visible start.

"What's wrong?" he asked, staring at her, his gray gaze narrowed into metallic sharpness.

Dinah said, "Nothing," very huskily.

"What is it about me that makes you freeze like that?" he burst out. "You were smiling when I came in—now you look as if you might run like blazes any minute. I don't usually have this effect on women."

"I'm sure you don't," Dinah said snappishly.

"There you go again, almost jumping down my throat at the slightest excuse." He eyed her with a controlled dislike which hardened his taut features. Dinah was thrown by that look. Her eyes wavered and fell to the polished surface of the table between them. Her own reflection gleamed mistily there, her smooth blond hair drawn back off her pale face and her white silk blouse merely a ghostly glimmer. She stared at herself without even knowing what she was seeing, remembering Greg's lazy smile and amused charm the day he arrived back from the States. It seemed a long time ago. Dinah wished vainly that she had not been so offhand with him from the start. He was Sir Gee's only son. One day he would run the firm. Not the man to make your enemy. Dinah, she thought, you are a fool.

Chapter Four

Lady Randal returned a few moments later to find her son and Dinah sitting in silence while the lightning flashed around the room. She exclaimed gently, switching on the table lamp, "What odd weather! I thought it felt very close this afternoon." To Dinah's relief she didn't appear to notice anything strange in the atmosphere apart from the sudden storm.

"Dinah, how are you going to get back to London? Shall I get Watson to make up a bed for you? You won't want to drive back in this weather, surely, though I'm sure we could find a car for you."

"I don't mind storms," Dinah said, flinching involuntarily as the thunder crashed overhead.

Greg laughed harshly under his breath. "So we see," he drawled coldly.

Dinah gave him a furious glance, and Lady Randal intercepted it, her brow creasing.

"Greg, you had better drive Dinah back if she wants to go." She looked at Dinah. "Although there's plenty of room, you know, and you're very welcome to stay. It was so kind of you to come down with my husband. He does get so steamed up in this sort of situation. He needs to let off some of that steam to someone."

Greg got up. "Right," he said, striding to the door. "I'll get my car."

"There's no need," Dinah began, and he turned back to give her a grim stare.

"I won't be a moment," he said through his teeth before vanishing.

"Have you and Greg quarreled over something?" Lady Randal asked in surprise, eying Dinah in a curious, probing way.

Dinah flushed. "Certainly not." You couldn't describe it as a quarrel, more of a long-distance feud, she thought.

"He's very sweet-tempered, really," his mother said fondly. "Much better tempered than his father."

With some people, maybe, Dinah thought. Not with me. With me he's difficult and always ready to snarl at the drop of a hat.

"Take no notice," Lady Randal soothed. "He'll come around. One thing you can say for Greg—he doesn't bear a grudge."

Oh, no? Dinah looked at her wryly. How well did she know her son? A mother was never the perfect guide to her son's behavior. She saw only his good side.

Lady Randal walked her to the door and kissed her cheek. "Thank you, Dinah, I appreciate you being there for Gee," she said warmly, with that famous smile. Yes, Greg had inherited that much, Dinah decided as she got into the car. He didn't exactly waste his smiles on Dinah, but she knew he could produce a smile like that when he saw fit to do so.

Rain was sluicing down as the car turned out of the drive, the windscreen wipers going very fast. Sliding a sideways look at her, Greg asked, "Sure you want to make the journey in this?"

"If it isn't inconvenient for you," Dinah said. "I could always get a taxi."

Greg's mouth tightened. "You annoy me, Miss Trevor."

Surprise, surprise, she thought. Who'd have thought it? And this was the sweet-tempered man who never bore a grudge, according to his fond mother? Which just went to show that she was right and mothers didn't know everything.

"Want to get back to town badly, do you?" he inquired in a curt tone.

"I want to get back," she agreed. She didn't have a thing to do when she did get back, but she didn't want to spend the night with the Randal family, not if Greg Randal was one of them. His parents she was fond of, but she couldn't stand the thought of being shut up in a house with him for a whole night.

He smiled as if his mouth were stiff. "Got a date, have you?" He didn't wait for her to answer that. "I wouldn't want to ruin your love life," he added nastily.

"Thank you," Dinah answered in a sweet voice.

He gave her a brief, narrow-eyed glare. "I'll keep my opinion to myself on the subject of people breaking up other people's marriages," he said through his teeth.

Dinah counted to ten. If she hadn't, she would have

said something pretty explosive. When she could trust herself to speak, she said calmly, "Before you form your opinions, you should make sure you have your facts straight."

"I think they're pretty accurate," he said, swinging around a corner at a terrific speed that made her heart leap into her mouth. "I can put two and two together," he added, putting his foot down on the accelerator and making the car jump forward with a roar. "Sometimes people are more obvious about things than they think they are."

She clutched the side of the seat with both hands, perspiration breaking out on her forehead. "Could you drive a little more slowly?" She made that a polite request, but her voice was shaking.

"Certainly," he flung at her, his speed not altering by a hair.

"It's only that I feel I'm too young to die," Dinah murmured. "You may not care if you end up in pieces all over the motorway, but I personally have a lot to live for."

"I'm sure you do," Greg muttered, slowing down at last. They overtook a small sports car and the driver gazed after them in fury as they shot past, the tires screeching on the wet road.

The storm was behind them now, a deep distant rumble of thunder accompanied by the occasional flash which split the cloudy sky all that remained of its former fury.

Greg was silent, and Dinah stared over the closely wooded landscape of the Weald of Kent. She tried to find the words to tell him he was wrong about her and

Andrew, but she had the impression he wouldn't believe her, whatever she said. Yet she decided, not knowing why, to try to explain.

"I've known Andrew since I was very small," she began, in a nervous, hesitant voice. She felt, rather than saw, Greg's head swing toward her and out of the corner of her eye she saw his long fingers gripping the wheel.

"We grew up together," Dinah added. "We're friends, that's all."

Greg laughed curtly. "Just good friends? That's a corny line, isn't it? Is that how his wife sees it?"

Dinah frowned. It had never occurred to her to wonder how Judy saw it. Judy knew that Andrew and Dinah had always been very close. Andrew had rushed Judy over to meet Dinah soon after he fell in love. Looking back, Dinah realized that somehow she and Judy had never become exactly friends, but Judy had always been polite to her, and welcoming if Dinah dropped in to see her.

"Judy realizes—" she began and Greg interrupted. "His wife has left him, hasn't she?"

"How did you know?" Dinah asked, surprised. Wondering just how much Greg knew.

"Everyone knows," Greg said with a clipped ring to his voice. "And everyone knows why."

Dinah turned to stare at him, her blue eyes enormous. "What do you mean?"

He turned, too, meeting her stare. "Don't play the innocent with me. Those big blue eyes are very deceptive. You know what I meant."

"I haven't got a clue," Dinah protested. Surely it wasn't common knowledge in the office that Judy wanted a divorce because she was in love with another man? Dinah couldn't believe that Andrew had gone around broadcasting the fact. Andrew had always chosen her as his confidante. He wasn't the type to talk easily to strangers or acquaintances.

"Oh, no, of course not," Greg said tightly, stepping up his speed again.

"Slow down," Dinah broke out. "This road could be a death trap in the rain."

"You make me so angry," he said, slowing. "The man's only been married a year, hasn't he? Couldn't you have given his unfortunate wife a chance? Why didn't he marry you in the first place if you've known him so long? Was it a sudden impulse on his part? Did he realize he had made a mistake almost at once? Or did you refuse to let him go?"

"You're crazy," Dinah muttered. "It isn't like that."

"Tell me what it *is* like," Greg demanded.

She was very angry by now, too. She didn't like the things he had said or the way he had said them. Why should she explain herself to him?

"You're not sitting in judgment on me," she told him with feverish irritation. "Mind your own business."

"Someone's got to make you see what a mess you're making of three lives," Greg told her forcefully.

"I'm not making a mess of anything," Dinah retorted. Why was she defending herself to this man? She would have liked to fling the truth at him, but she had no right to repeat what Andrew had told her. Andrew's pride would be crushed if everyone in the firm knew that his wife had left him for another man so soon after their marriage. Andrew was calm and even-tempered on the surface, but every man has a deep desire to retain his ego undented. Andrew's had been in a bad way lately. He didn't begin to understand Judy and he was curiously weak when it came to managing women.

They were coming into the grimy London suburbs. Slate roofs shone in the rain. The streets of shabby gray houses stretched on either side. Traffic thickened and slowed around them, and Greg had to bring his speed down to a jerking crawl. It didn't do much for his temper. At a traffic light he drummed his long fingers on the wheel, his eyes fixed on the taillights of the car in front of them.

"I can't understand a girl with looks like yours getting into a situation like that," he muttered. "What do you see in him?"

"Andrew is an old friend," Dinah said, watching his fingers tap out that restless, impatient rhythm. "That's all. Just an old friend, nothing more."

"Tell that to the marines," Greg said, his car jerking into motion as the lights changed and the line of traffic began to move forward.

He dropped her outside her flat without another word. When Dinah opened the front door, Dilly was standing at the window, staring out with a distraught expression. She swung around to stare at Dinah, breaking out, "Why didn't he come in?"

"He drove me up from Kent," Dinah told her. "His grandmother has had a stroke. I went down there with Sir Gee and Greg drove me home. He has to get back there, though."

"He could have come in to say hello," Dilly wailed, running a hand through her curls. "It wouldn't have taken a minute." She bolted off to the bathroom and locked herself in while Jennifer and Dinah stared at each other in grim silence, with a look of "here we go again" on their faces.

"She'll have to go," Jennifer said after a pause.

"Why does she react like that?" Dinah was in no mood to be patient with Dilly's emotional storms today. "She has a long way to go before she makes it to adolescence. She should never have left school. She wasn't ready for the big world."

Jennifer laughed. "Poor Dilly." She sobered, eying Dinah. "Is Sir George's mother seriously ill?"

Dinah shook her head. "Not really. The last I heard, she and Sir Gee were having a nasty squabble, and if she were really ill he wouldn't pick quarrels with her."

"Didn't you say she was over ninety, though?" Dinah began to laugh, nodding, and Jennifer stared at her in surprise. "What's funny?"

"I'm sorry," Dinah said, surprised herself to find tears in her eyes. "I'm a bit distraught. It was a shock."

"Did you know her that well? I'd no idea," Jennifer said, staring in a funny way.

Flushed, Dinah moved to the door. "She's rather a dear," she evaded as she went to her own room.

Dilly's reaction to Greg had bothered her. How often had Dilly seen him since the night he dropped in here for his father's speech? Dilly was an oddly faithful soul. Hamish took up all her attention when he was around. But when Hamish abandoned her she turned in a desperate way to the first friendly male who came within a foot of her. Dilly hated to spend time alone. She had such extreme amounts of emotion to spend and she had to pour them out on a man. Not Greg Randal, though, Dinah told herself. He wasn't a safe object for Dilly's riotous emotions.

Come back, Hamish, all is forgiven, she thought, dropping onto her bed and lying there in a lazy attitude with her eyes fixed on the ceiling.

Greg, in a different way, was another Hamish, but far more dangerous, because he was far more sophisticated and far less likely to take Dilly seriously.

He might take her, though, on a whim, and Dilly could get hurt. "Over my dead body," Dinah said through her teeth. "I'll kill him if he hurts that idiotic girl." Dilly might be infuriating, but Dinah was fond of her. She wouldn't have her hurt for worlds.

For a man who felt free to express contempt and disapproval over someone else's private life, Greg Randal was certainly very casual about how he affected others.

Jennifer strolled past the door an hour later in a ravishing green dress and stopped to say that Dilly was still in the bathroom.

"I'm off in a minute," she added. "Try to get her out while I'm gone. I don't want to find her still there in the morning. It isn't easy to wash at the kitchen sink, you know."

"Who is it tonight?" Dinah asked without real interest. All Jennifer's men looked the same to her. She liked them with money and good manners, but she didn't seem to require much in the way of brains. They tended to be inarticulate and prone to smiling without any apparent cause.

"No one special," Jennifer said casually.

The doorbell went and she shot off without another word. Dinah came out, too, and saw a tall, fair-haired man at the door. She caught the briefest glimpse of him before he vanished in Jennifer's wake. His voice floated back to her, though.

"I thought we'd take in a play, actually."

As Jennifer had said, he was no one special. Dinah could tell that from his smooth, bland, empty voice. What did Jennifer want with men like that? What did she see in them? She was an intelligent girl and an ambitious one. Dinah couldn't fathom what she was looking for in a man. It was certainly not intelligence, anyway. Maybe it was money? Dinah sighed. Jennifer wouldn't be so silly, surely. Money might make life smoother, but it couldn't make it happier.

Dilly sidled out soon afterward, avoiding Dinah's eyes. She had been crying again and her eyes were red and puffy. Dinah felt a twinge of anger mixed with pity and irritation, but it was her fondness for Dilly which won in the end.

"You are an idiot," she told her. What use was there in scolding her? Dilly was half a little girl, even if a precocious one. People don't progress from childhood to adulthood in one stride. They zigzag back and forth—one minute five years old, the next entirely mature. You have to be tolerant with the swings and roundabouts of adolescence. Dinah looked back over her own and sighed. She had been there. She remembered it all too well. It wasn't so long ago, and, she had to admit, her own behavior hadn't been much less erratic than Dilly's. Dinah had been less blatant about it, that was all. She had tried to hide her emotional volatility. Dilly didn't even try. Maybe she couldn't. Maybe hers was the only way she knew. But she'd have to change to make it in the world.

So Dinah smiled at Dilly wryly. "Come on, let's

make some coffee," she offered. "You can tell me all about it."

Perched on a stool, Dilly poured it all out. Dinah didn't interrupt. She listened. All Dilly wanted was an ear, a sympathetic ear.

"What's wrong with me? Why do men refuse to take me seriously?" That was what she wanted to know. "I can't keep a man, however hard I try. No matter what I do, it doesn't matter."

"Perhaps you shouldn't try so hard," Dinah suggested, but then wished she hadn't said that because it made Dilly's tear ducts start to work again.

"You'll make yourself ill," Dinah soothed. "Drink your coffee." What had happened between Dilly and Greg Randal? she wondered. Surely he must have seen how emotionally insecure Dilly was?

"I love him," Dilly sobbed, and Dinah was angry with Greg Randal for encouraging her. Of course, it didn't mean anything. Dilly's eager emotion went out to anyone ready to give her a kind word. She was a stray dog looking for a good home. She needed to be protected from herself. Dinah wished she knew how to get it home to Dilly that she was damaging herself with this wild excess of feeling.

She talked quietly, hoping that Dilly was listening. It was no good getting angry with Dilly. "It's good advice," Dinah said. "Believe me, Dilly. You must stop rushing at people and trying to make them love you. You can't do that. It scares them off."

"Yes," Dilly said, hiccuping.

Did she agree? Or was she just making those resigned gulps because she was worn out with her crying jag and had no more tears to shed?

"Be patient. Love will come. You can't force it." I ought to be editing an agony column, Dinah told herself. I'm good. A pity I don't take my own advice. It's so much easier to give advice than take it, though, and I can never quite convince myself the way I convince others. *I* know what a fool I am.

In bed that night she lay thinking about Greg Randal. It hurt to know how low his opinion of her was; she wished she could tell him the truth about Andrew, but how could she?

She could ask Andrew if he would mind, of course. She thought of broaching the subject but knew she would never do it. What on earth could she say to him?

It was a tangled mess. She barely knew Greg Randal and he was of no importance to her. Was he? A flush crept up her face. She stiffened in the bed, biting her lip. Of course he wasn't. Why should he be?

Andrew was important, though. She had known him for most of her life and she was very fond of him. Andrew was having a bad time, and Dinah could not make it worse by telling him what Greg Randal thought about their relationship. It would embarrass Andrew. It would make him avoid her, and Andrew needed a sympathetic ear every bit as much as Dilly did. Oh, what a confusing situation this was turning out to be.

I need one, too, thought Dinah. I wish I had a sympathetic ear. She could never bring herself to confide her private feelings to people, though. She preferred to keep them locked up inside herself.

When she went to work the next morning she found Greg in his father's office. Dinah halted in the doorway, staring, and Greg looked up from the papers he was studying to give her a look of sardonic impatience.

"It's becoming a habit."

Dinah slowly walked forward, the opened letters in her hand. "What is?"

"Unpunctuality."

Her face took on a faint pink. "I missed my train," she admitted, then flared in sudden irritation. "I'm only five minutes behind time, though. Sir Gee doesn't arrive for ten minutes."

"Today he isn't coming at all."

Dinah looked at him incredulously. "Not coming? Sir Gee?"

"He's taken a day off," Greg said, smiling in sudden amusement. "He's down at St. Mark with my grandmother. They haven't finished their argument."

Dinah laughed, and their eyes met and held in shared amusement. It was a strange brief interlude in the hectic day which followed. Dinah had often wondered what it would be like to work with Greg Randal instead of his father, and now she found out. It was different, certainly. The pace didn't slacken, however. Greg, she found, was every bit as demanding, rapid and overbearing. He worked at a speed which left her breathless, despite her training with Sir Gee.

They had a working lunch in the office. Dinah sent out for sandwiches and they shared them over the desk together.

The phone rang and Greg snatched it up, talking impatiently, his face averted from her. Dinah watched him, her eyes moving over that strong profile. His skin still retained a lingering tan, the smooth golden gleam of it accentuating his hard bone structure. His lids were down over those gray eyes, but as he spoke his lashes flickered restlessly and his mouth moved in a faint smile. He's far too attractive, Dinah thought irritably. She wished it weren't giving her pleasure to look at him, but she couldn't hide from herself that she found it impossible not to look at him. No wonder all the girls in the office tumbled at his feet when he gave them that quick smile.

He flashed a glance at her, and she hurriedly looked away as though afraid of what he might see in her eyes. Greg Randal wasn't adding her to his list of adoring victims. Dinah had been immunized against his sort of charm when she was eighteen and she had no intention of falling prey to it again.

"Get that Paris file, will you?" he asked out of the corner of his mouth.

Dinah found it and came back to put it in front of him. As she bent he half turned and their cheeks brushed. Dinah shot back like a stung cat and Greg's gray eyes took on a hard glint.

He didn't say anything, but he had noticed her movement and he didn't like it.

What is the matter with me? Dinah asked herself furiously, going back to her chair and bending her blond head over her sheaf of papers. I'm behaving like Dilly, for heaven's sake, and Greg Randal isn't going to miss that. He's far too quick, far too intelligent. He knows the effect he has on women. He'll leap to all the wrong conclusions.

She looked at him through her lashes and found him staring at her. Nervously, Dinah shifted her gaze elsewhere. I must stop looking at him, she told herself. Nothing has changed. I'm immune to men like that.

She had seen Greg smiling at other women. She knew what value to put on one of his charming smiles. Common sense dictated that she should keep a distance between them.

Greg hung up and sat there, staring at the file. "I'm going to have to go over myself," he said under his breath. "Blast."

"Go where?" She looked at the file. "Paris?"

He nodded. "There's far too much at stake to risk any mistakes at this stage. The decision has to be made on the spot." Looking up, he ran his hand through his thick black hair, smoothing it down. It was a gesture he often made. Dinah watched it intently. The sunlight falling through the window beside him gave his hair a blue-black gleam. Their eyes met and she looked away.

"What's gone wrong?" She hoped her voice sounded steady. Her breathing had suddenly gone crazy. She didn't know why it should make her heart miss a beat whenever those gray eyes touched her. Why did he affect her so? I'm going out of my mind, she told herself. That's what's wrong.

"The design team are arguing about the alterations to the new block. If we're going to move in next spring they'll have to get a move on, but they can't make up their minds." The newly acquired block had been in use as offices before, but a good deal of alteration would be required before they were suitable for the Randal organization. Dinah knew that the number of offices would have to be increased, which meant a lot of interior redesigning.

"When will you go?"

Greg shrugged. "As soon as my father comes back."

"Shall I make the arrangements?" She caught herself up. "I expect your secretary will be doing that, though."

Greg tapped his long fingers on the desk thoughtfully. "No," he murmured, not looking at her. "You do it. You had better come, too."

Dinah had half risen to go and check flight times. She stayed there, her mouth open.

Greg gave her a sardonic look. She slowly sat down again and said weakly, "Come with you? Me?"

"I'm going to need your memory for detail. You've been in on the Paris deal from the start. I'm coming to it cold and my secretary doesn't know a thing about it either. I'll have to know all there is so nothing can go wrong. You'll have to come to feed me the facts."

"What facts?" Dinah asked practically, her nerve ends quivering with suspicion. He didn't need her. He was just saying that. All he needed was the dossier on the Paris operation.

"I can't carry figures around in my head," he said, then gave her a wicked, mocking grin. "Well, not that sort, anyway."

Dinah's blue eyes iced over. She knew the sort of figures he found easiest to remember.

"All you need is the dossier," she pointed out, looking at the bulging folder in front of him.

"I prefer to have a walking computer with me," he mocked, leaning toward her with his hands flat on the desk and his gray eyes deliberately teasing her.

"I'm flattered," she said through her teeth. A walking computer, was she? Charming. What a delightful man he was when he chose. He managed to make a compliment sound like a deadly insult, and maybe it was—who wanted to be described as a walking computer?

"I'll discuss it with my father," Greg said, which left her with no shred of an excuse. She could hardly claim that she couldn't go if Sir Gee ordered her to.

Greg knew that. He gave her another of his smiles, reckless amusement in his eyes. "My father's desperate to get this scheme off the ground and into good working order as soon as possible," he told her, as if she didn't already know that. Sir Gee liked to get things moving; he hated wasting time. Everything he did was done at a terrific speed. And Greg wanted to reinforce the fact that she would have to go with him.

"We'll only need a couple of days there," Greg murmured. "My father will survive without you for that long."

But would she survive two days in Paris alone with Greg Randal? Dinah asked herself. She found it difficult enough to be in the same office with him now. Odd things kept happening to her pulse rate. She didn't want to notice the way his hard mouth could curve into a sudden smile. She didn't want to notice the mocking gleam in his gray eyes. But she couldn't stop herself. What was happening to her?

"It won't bother you, will it?" Greg said, far too softly, watching her, his gaze running from the elegantly brushed blond hair over her troubled face, speculation in his scrutiny.

"No," Dinah said, because she would die rather than let him guess it bothered her far too much.

"You often go on business trips with my father, don't

you?" Greg pointed out, and she nodded. She had flown all over the world with Sir Gee. He didn't like to have to get his facts from dossiers, either. He liked to have her on tap when he needed to know something and he needed to have someone he could trust to make arrangements, find out anything he needed to know and Dinah was the person he counted on for that.

"Your passport is in order?"

She nodded.

"So where's the problem?" probed Greg, still watching her like a cat at a mousehole.

"No problem," Dinah said very brightly, smiling with the last ounce of her self-control.

"Good." Greg smiled back. "Make the arrangements for us, then, will you? My father should be back tomorrow. He's too much of a work addict to stay away any longer."

"I'll make sure the arrangements are made," Dinah said without emotion.

Dinah got up and Greg said smoothly, "I hope Duncan won't miss you too much."

She ignored that, walking out with her blond head in the air. In fact, she was having dinner with Andrew. He had rung her during the morning and pleaded for help.

He picked her up outside the office and drove her to a quiet restaurant where they had a leisurely drink while Andrew poured out the latest twist in his marriage problem.

"I've heard from Judy's lawyer." He played with his glass, frowning at the amber liquid with intense concentration.

"She really means to go through with it?" Dinah asked, shaken, because she hadn't quite believed Judy would do it.

He nodded, pushing his glass around on the bar counter. "It will take time, of course, but she's set things in motion."

"I'm sorry, Andrew," Dinah murmured anxiously.

"If only I could see her, talk to her . . . I can't believe I couldn't get her to change her mind. I know we've quarreled from time to time, but in other ways our marriage was very good." His quiet voice had a dry, weary sound to it. He looked as if he hadn't slept for days. He looked ill. You could see all the pain welling up inside him.

"I wish there was something I could do," Dinah muttered. She hated to see him in such a state.

He looked up, pleading in his eyes. "See her, Dinah. Will you? Will you talk to her? Find out what's gone wrong between us and who this other guy is—if I find out I'll strangle him with my bare hands; I swear I will." There was rage in his eyes, and that was astonishing because Andrew had such a quiet, gentle temperament. But she guessed there were some things that could alter a person's attitude totally.

"If she'll see me," Dinah said dubiously. She and Judy had never been very close. She had tried to make friends with Judy, but somehow, however polite Judy was, she seemed very distant. She hadn't wanted to admit Dinah to her friendship.

"I'm sure she will," Andrew said trustingly. Smiling at her, he said, "You're so marvelous with people. You can talk to them. I can't. I never know what to say. That was a lot of the trouble with Judy—I couldn't get through to her when she was in one of her moods. She'd never listen to me."

Whenever Judy was difficult, Andrew had run to Dinah and poured all his troubles out to her.

"I find it easy to talk to you," he would say. "We've known each other so long. I don't have to think how to say things. You know what I mean. You always understand."

It was nice to hear that, but it was worrying, too, because Andrew should be able to talk to his own wife without asking Dinah to intervene. A good marriage doesn't need an interpreter. It has its own internal communication lines. Was Andrew's marriage worth saving? Dinah looked at his unhappy, worried face and sighed. Andrew loved Judy, even if he couldn't talk to her. Surely there must be a way to get them back together again?

"How do I find her?" she asked, and Andrew's face lit up with gratitude and hope.

"Her parents," he said. "They know where she is—but they won't tell me. They might tell you, though."

"I'll go around and see them," Dinah promised. "It will have to be when I get back from Paris, though," she added. "I leave tomorrow afternoon, and there's a lot to do before I go."

"I heard there was some sort of hitch," Andrew said, because of course the office grapevine worked like a dream and everyone knew what was happening in the firm.

"Quarreling among the designers," she told him.

He nodded. "So I gather." Andrew was a good executive; he took things calmly.

"Is Sir Gee going?" he asked her over dinner, and she looked up warily to shake her head and tell him she was going with Greg Randal.

Andrew laughed, looking surprised and amused. "That will make the other girls green with envy. He's a very popular guy with them."

"A wanted man," Dinah said through her teeth, and Andrew stared at her in surprise at her barbed tone.

"Don't you like him?"

"I'm not joining his fan club just yet," Dinah said, then changed the subject to ask about his family. "How are they? I haven't seen them for ages."

It got them off the subject of Greg Randal and his name didn't crop up again all evening, for which Dinah was thankful. She was trying not to think about him any more than she could help. He was a thorn in her flesh. He disturbed her, and Dinah did not like being disturbed by any man. She had too much pride and placed too high a value on her peace of mind. Greg Randal threatened both.

Andrew drove her back to the flat at around eleven and parked outside, leaning back with his eyes closed. "Gee, I'm tired."

"Haven't been sleeping?" Dinah had guessed as much and she was troubled by the drawn and haggard face which was so unlike Andrew's usually cheerful appearance.

He nodded. "I hate taking sleeping pills, but I may have to ask my doctor for some. How can I work when I'm not getting any sleep?"

"You can't," Dinah said bluntly. Andrew would crack up if he kept on like this—and Dinah was suddenly angry with Judy for getting him into this condition. She had married him, for heaven's sake. Why didn't she care what was happening to him? Marriage was a serious commitment, not a game. Judy had apparently never taken her marriage vows seriously or she couldn't behave like this. Andrew was the sort of man who needed a wife behind him all the time. He didn't have any fire and energy of his own. He was such a gentle person, though, and took every aspect of life so soberly. He deserved better than this from Judy.

He lifted his shoulders in a tired shrug. "What can I do?"

You could fight it, Dinah thought, but didn't say so because she knew him too well. Andrew was a slow, patient man, but he wasn't the type to fight with fierce determination. He put too low a value on himself. He gave in too easily; he backed down too soon. He should have given Judy cause to take him more seriously; but then, if he had, he wouldn't be Andrew, he would be some other man.

Greg Randal wouldn't let his wife run off with another man without moving heaven and earth to find her and bring her back, Dinah thought, making a face. Greg might be maddening, he might be dangerously charming, but he had his father's fire and energy, and no woman could ever hope to run rings around Greg Randal. He wouldn't stand still for it.

"I must go in," she told Andrew, smiling affectionately at him. "When you get home, have some cocoa and go to bed and don't think about Judy. I'll see her and sort it out if I can."

"What would I do without you?" Andrew said with a deep, wrenching sigh.

Dinah let herself into the flat and found the living room in semidarkness. Only a table lamp gave faint light. There was slow, romantic music on the record player, and on the couch sat Dilly, wearing a vivid green dress and a dreamy expression, curled up close to Greg Randal, her eyes fixed adoringly on him.

Dinah halted, rage flaring in her veins. Greg's cool stare flashed down over her, but Dilly was too lost in a dream world even to look up.

"Took a long time getting out of his car, didn't you?" Greg asked in barbed sarcasm.

How did he know that? Dinah's brows jerked together. Had he been spying from the window? And what was he doing here at this hour? What had put that glazed expression into Dilly's eyes?

Ignoring his question, she looked at her watch. "It's half past eleven."

"So?" Greg drawled, putting up a hand to brush Dilly's untidy curls back from her face.

"Dilly should be in bed."

Dilly heard that. She looked up indignantly, red color running up her face. "I'll say when I go to bed," she retorted.

"Who asked you to run her life for her?" Greg demanded in smiling impatience. "She's not a child."

That's just what she is, Dinah thought, looking with dismay at Dilly's excited eyes, and you are no good for her, Greg Randal. Dilly was busy throwing herself at him, and Greg Randal was never going to be other than amused by her. He was almost twice her age, for a start, and highly sophisticated. Dilly was providing him with a little fun tonight, but it wasn't just fun to Dilly. It was romance, excitement, glamor; and when Greg got bored and wandered away, Dilly was going to come down from her dream cloud with a thump which would be heard from one end of London to the other.

I know who's going to have to pick up the pieces, too, Dinah thought grimly. I know who's going to have to winkle her out of the bathroom when she's sobbing her heart out into the hot water. Hamish was bad enough, but Greg Randal is going to break her into tiny pieces.

She looked at him in glacial dislike and found him looking back at her in much the same way.

"Dilly has to get up in the morning," Dinah pointed out.

Greg rose, his impressive height almost making her back off in alarm. He stalked past her in menacing silence and slammed out of the flat.

"I hate you," Dilly yelled, leaping off the couch, too, and running toward her own room. "Why don't you mind your own business?"

Staring after her, Dinah asked herself why she didn't do just that. It was no easy role to play—that of busybody. Nobody liked you. Why didn't she just let Dilly run headlong into disaster? Why did she feel it her job to protect Dilly?

Switching off the record player and then the lamp, she made her way into the bathroom. She regarded herself in the mirror with wry displeasure. Mind your own business, Dinah Trevor, she told the reflection. If Dilly wants to get her heart broken all over again, let her. It's not your business, anyway. But she knew she couldn't just stand back and watch while Dilly went through another wild emotional trauma. Dinah couldn't stand aside when someone she loved was getting hurt. All her instincts were to stop it before it got worse—and if she knew anything about me, Greg Randal was going to be far worse for Dilly than Hamish had ever been.

Chapter Five

They flew in to Charles de Gaulle Airport on the following afternoon and found Paris bathed in a pale sunlight which gave beauty even to the drab outskirts of the city as they drove toward it along the autoroute into the center of the city. The volume of traffic was extremely heavy. Cars swerved all around them, horns blaring, tires screeching, and Dinah nervously tried to ignore Greg's brooding presence beside her in the back of the taxi.

He had barely spoken on the flight, his black head bent over a French newspaper which had been provided by the stewardess on the plane. Dinah had accepted a London daily and pretended to be engrossed in that, but she had been aware of Greg in the next seat all the time, his every little movement drawing her attention.

She couldn't understand how it had grown up inside

her—this queer, prickling awareness of him. It had been easy for her to walk wary of men like Greg Randal in the past. Her common sense had told her how much value to place on male charm: none. She didn't want to be fooled into false relationships. Dinah had always told herself that she preferred men she could trust. Sex appeal didn't count for much with her. But she couldn't hide from herself any longer that she was finding it very hard to shut off her own instinctive physical reactions to Greg Randal.

I don't even like him, she told herself, wondering if she were going crazy. She had always believed that she was too sane to feel a purely physical attraction for a man she didn't like, yet every time Greg came near her she found herself fighting for breath. She might still be able to disguise it from him behind a cool smile, but she could no longer disguise it from herself.

She had spent the whole flight scolding herself. From all that she had heard about him she could guess that any relationship with Greg was bound to be short-lived, and Dinah had no intention whatever of getting into one of those brief, painful affairs. Greg Randal might be able to smile his way through a love affair, but Dinah took life far too seriously. She could only get hurt; and she didn't want that. She wasn't going to let him do that to her.

All you have to do is hide it from him, she told herself, and hide it from yourself, too. It will pass. Time heals everything. It isn't the end of the world. So you fancy him? Refuse to give in to it. It's easy. You can do it.

Dinah could give other people wise advice, but

somehow she couldn't get herself to listen. Sexual attraction isn't responsive to calm thinking. Sanity can't touch it. It moves in its own circle of cause and effect, and Dinah knew that the only way she was going to be able to banish Greg Randal from her mind was by staying out of his way, which wasn't going to be easy, having to spend this time with him in Paris.

Their hotel was on the far side of the Place Vendôme, close to the beautiful Tuileries Gardens. The taxi shot past the green column from which Napoleon, in a laurel wreath and toga, gazed with ineffable satisfaction, and drew up with a jerk outside the wide hotel entrance.

A doorman in gleaming livery hurried to help Dinah out of the taxi and onto the pavement. Greg paid the driver, his long-limbed body bent forward as he talked. The wind raked his black hair and blew it into crisp disorder. Dinah stood watching him with intent eyes. He was far too attractive, she thought grimly. As he straightened Dinah quickly turned away to walk into the hotel.

Greg drew level with her in a few strides. The wide foyer was almost empty, but the blond receptionist gave Greg a welcoming smile, speaking English with a distinct American accent.

Dinah wandered toward the lifts. A cocktail bar opened off the foyer, and Dinah paused to listen as the sound of ragtime drifted from it. A lady in a red dress was playing the piano with verve and energy, her head nodding in time to the beat. The customers sipped at their drinks and talked in low voices.

"We're free this evening," Greg said behind her,

making Dinah start and look around. "What would you like to do?"

Dinah dragged her mind back from the thoughts which had been occupying it. "Do?" she repeated vaguely, frowning.

"We could have dinner here in the hotel," Greg suggested. "Or we could go out into Paris and find somewhere to eat."

Dinah hesitated. She was reluctant to spend any time alone with him. It was far too dangerous in her unsettled state of mind.

Greg's hard mouth twisted in a snarl. "Sorry if neither prospect turns you on, but you'll have to put up with me for the next few days, won't you? We'll go out." Having settled that to his own satisfaction, he strode past her into the lift, behind the porter who was carrying their luggage.

In her room later Dinah sat on the edge of the bed staring at herself in the dressing-table mirror. She was brushing her hair slowly, trying to think. Her mind had become oddly disorganized lately. She wasn't used to it, usually she was in complete control of herself. Her thoughts seeped out of it every time she tried to pin them down.

Her long blond hair streamed down over her bare shoulders and framed her face in a pale gold shimmer. Her blue eyes had lost their normal calm look. Her smooth skin was flushed and her mouth wasn't quite steady.

She felt depressed. She was not looking forward to spending an evening alone with Greg Randal. It was becoming difficult for her to talk to him. She was far too aware of him and having more of a struggle than she would have expected to hide it from him.

She stood up and moved away, her nylon slip crackling with electricity. She felt that she was charged with electricity herself. It tingled in her skin. She felt that if she flicked her fingers sparks would fly from them. Why did she feel this way?

She had brought a plain black dress for evening wear. It had a simple scooped neckline and filmy sleeves which belled out at the elbow and were clipped around her wrist, giving the dress a faintly medieval look.

She clipped her hair behind her neck with a wide diamanté bow. It looked less formal like that and made her feel good when she anxiously inspected her own reflection before going down to meet Greg.

He was in the bar, sipping a sherry. Walking toward him, Dinah couldn't meet his eyes. She pretended to be looking around the crowded room, which meant that she saw only too clearly how much female interest was focused on Greg. His lean dark figure was the center of attention for every woman in the place.

She sank down on the couch beside him, her throat dry with nerves.

"What will you have to drink?" Greg sat down again after having risen courteously to acknowledge her arrival.

Dinah flickered a look at his drink. "The same, please."

He crooked a finger and the waiter sprang to his side, smiling.

Greg got that sort of service. Dinah had noticed before that some men always managed to get personal attention wherever they went. It wasn't just his money that made waiters jump to his call; it was that cool confidence of his—Greg expected to get what he wanted, so he got it.

"You look very beautiful," he murmured in a low voice, his eyes fixed on her.

"Thank you." She almost put a hand to her throat to hide from him the pulse which began beating there at his intimate tone.

He looked very good himself in a smoothly tailored dark evening suit, his wide shoulders accentuated by the well-cut jacket. His thick black hair was brushed carefully and his hard features were almost relaxed as he smiled at her. His beautiful gray eyes were accentuated by his dark clothing.

"Can't we have a truce for tonight?" She saw lazy charm in his gray eyes. "Must we spend every minute of the day sniping at each other?"

Warily, Dinah smiled back. She certainly didn't want to have an endless duel on her hands. "Where are we going?" she asked, and Greg told her he had booked a table at a famous Paris nightspot.

"I thought we might as well go out on the town. They have a very good floor show, I'm told."

The waiter brought her drink and drifted away. Dinah sipped at the sherry, listening to the soft whisper of music coming from a loudspeaker over on the other side of the room, the pianist having taken a break.

"Do you know Paris well?" Greg asked, and she shrugged, turning her blond head to smile at him.

"I've been here once or twice. What about you?"

"The same," he said. "But I did spend a year studying here when I was eighteen. My father wanted me to be bilingual—if you can speak both English and

French you can travel almost anywhere in the world and be understood."

"Your father doesn't need languages," Dinah told him, beginning to laugh. "He gets by without words." Sir Gee could communicate with a look. He always managed to make himself understood no matter who he was talking to.

Greg slanted his gaze toward her, mockery in his smile. "You manage it, too. I don't need to be told in words what you think of me—you make it all too obvious."

"Do I?" That was reassuring. She looked at him, her face blandly vague. From his tone she could see that he didn't have a clue to what he was doing to her, and Dinah found that quite a relief.

"You can take me or leave me, right?" He was talking with a smile, as though the idea amused him. It certainly didn't bother him. She was glad about that, too. The last thing she wanted was for Greg Randal to guess how she was beginning to feel. That would make her feel an even bigger fool than she felt now.

"I've never got such a definite thumbs-down signal from anyone," he said lightly. "I must be slipping."

"You can't win them all," she offered brightly, pinning a smile to her face and hoping it wouldn't slip.

"Obviously," he agreed, his mouth twisting.

"You have plenty of other fans," Dinah said sweetly. "I hear your fan club singing a chorus of praise in the canteen every time I'm there."

"But you don't join them," Greg murmured, studying his glass as though it fascinated him.

Dinah didn't answer that, and after a moment he went on. "Dilly tells me you're very particular about your men. She wishes she knew your secret. She says you're stylish, a very cool lady, and you never get into a state about anyone. She admires you, you know."

Dinah laughed, surprised. "She's told you more than she's ever told me, then."

"Maybe I shouldn't have told you. She may not want you to know. She's a funny kid." He paused, smiling. "Cute, though." He rose as she finished her sherry. "Shall we go?"

They had dinner, as he had promised, at one of the most famous of Parisian nightclubs. The food was well cooked and elegantly served, the wine was excellent, but it was the floor show which brought the visitors flooding in each night. There were lots of girls in feathers and very little else, several fast-talking comedians who switched effortlessly to English or German when they heard the audience speaking one or the other and some jugglers who did the most incredible things with a wide variety of objects from metal rings to plates.

Dinah was grateful for the floor show. It helped to pass the time safely. She could pretend she had forgotten Greg and concentrate on what was happening on the small stage. Of course, she didn't really forget him for a second. She knew he was there, all right. Only too well. She heard every breath he took and felt his every little movement intensely, more than she wanted to.

On the whole, the evening was a success. Somehow she and Greg walked the tightrope of polite harmony without either of them slipping for a second. Dinah ransacked her mind for small talk which wouldn't destroy their fragile truce. Greg did the same. They discussed the firm, Sir Gee, Paris, France and the

Common Market. When they had run through that lot
they went through them again in different words. It was
very wearing, but they managed it, all without the
slightest bit of belligerence.

When the floor show ended things got rather more
difficult. They sat at their table with glasses of champagne and stared at the tablecloth with as much apparent absorption as if it had a secret message woven into
the threads. Dinah couldn't lift her eyes. The champagne had got into her bloodstream and she was weak
at the knees. Through her eyelashes, she could see
Greg's brown hand curled around the stem of his
wineglass. She couldn't take her eyes off those long,
powerful fingers. A fierce sexual attraction was beating
in her veins, and she knew she wouldn't be able to hide
it if Greg really looked at her.

He drained his glass suddenly. "It's late," he said, in
a voice which sounded harsh and abrupt.

Dinah stumbled to her feet. I'm not drunk, am I? she
asked herself, trying to walk steadily to the exit through
the crowded tables. The band was playing muted
romantic music. It didn't exactly help. As they walked
out the music floated after them and twined itself
around Dinah's ears. She heard it all the way back to
the hotel. The taxi drove along the Seine in the brilliant
lamplight. There were great crowds still wandering the
Paris night, especially around the Latin Quarter, which
was open half the night.

Dinah looked sideways and saw the oily black water
of the river shining under the artificial lighting from the
river bank. One of the *bateaux-de-mouches* went by in a
blaze of electricity with the voice of the guide drifting in
its wake: "*Et voici, messieurs, mesdames, Notre*

Dame . . ." Looking back, Dinah saw the cathedral with a cloudy sky behind it. The formal façade had a stiff look by night, the carved figures of kings marching along the front.

The district surrounding their hotel was an exclusive area of haute couture shops and jewelry stores where the prices were never mentioned, let alone displayed. If you needed to ask, you couldn't afford it. At night the streets were silent and empty. The classical architecture shimmered under the full moon, which came and went behind the clouds. Across the street in the Tuileries Gardens a quiet wind rustled the trees and blew the spray from the great fountains across the graveled paths.

Dinah waited as Greg paid the taxi driver, staring around her. She didn't feel much like going to bed. Her senses were extremely awake. She was both dreamy and excited.

Greg looked down at her as he turned. In the dark street his eyes gleamed like gray stones. "Feel like a walk before bed?" Could he have read her mind?

Dinah was tempted, but she was still too cautious to give in to temptation. "I'm tired," she claimed, turning away.

"Tired? Or scared?" Greg asked softly at her back, and she walked hurriedly into the hotel. There had been a mocking intimacy in his voice which left her breathless. She felt she had to get away from him before she betrayed herself.

She reminded herself that he was a flirt. She had heard him teasing other girls in the office in a warm, smiling voice and heard them stammering replies, only too obviously reduced to incoherence by that lazy charm. Greg Randal was an expert at that game. He knew how to light a fire in three easy stages. Not with me, though, Dinah thought rebelliously. He isn't lighting any fire for me. I'm not going to fall into his trap and start playing his game.

The lift stood open as they approached it. Greg pressed the button for their floor and the doors closed. Leaning against the wall opposite her, Greg openly studied her, his hands thrust into his pockets and his long, lean body at ease.

Dinah didn't even look at him. She fixed her eyes on the floor and saw the black toecaps of his shoes instead. When the lift stopped she drew a startled breath and moved forward.

Greg followed her into the corridor. Dinah fumbled for her door key, still trying to evade his watchful gaze.

It took her a full minute to open her door. The lock appeared to resist all attempts to shift it. She was trembling by the time she had finally managed it.

"Good night," she muttered, getting ready to bolt.

When Greg's hands descended on her shoulders her body stiffened and she gave a quite audible intake of breath.

"Don't," she whispered hoarsely, pulling away.

Greg didn't say a word, but his fingers tightened and refused to release her. She was dragged against him, struggling, and his head came down to shut out the light.

For one more second Dinah resisted the heated pressure of his lips; then she weakly surrendered, the blood beating in her ears and deafening her. Her hands lay against his hard chest, the heavy thud of his heart beating under her palms. She had lost the ability to think. She was melting, burning, her mouth crushed under that hard, fierce demand.

If she hadn't been past thinking, Dinah would have been telling herself in dazed confusion that nothing like this had ever happened to her before. It was the first time in her whole life that she had absolutely lost her cool. She was dissolving in Greg Randal's arms, trembling like a leaf against him, feeling the sensual glide of his fingers up and down her spine, entirely responsive to those exploring movements.

Then Greg pulled his head back, with a long, harsh intake of breath. Under her hands his heart beat an overfast tattoo. His face was very flushed.

Her own breathing was in a bad way, too. Her head was flung back in yielding surrender, and as her eyes slowly fluttered open they focused on him without seeing him too well. Greg's face was a darker shadow against the intrusive light which made her blink.

"That's more like it," he said huskily, with a grim satisfaction which acted on her like the touch of acid.

Dinah was blazingly angry in a flash. His tone, his smile, made her come awake with a vengeance. Greg was pleased with himself. He thought he had won. The Randal magic had claimed another helpless victim. Well, he could think again. She did not want to be his prey.

"More like what?" she inquired with a honey-sweet coldness. "Or should I say, more like *who?*"

His eyes narrowed abruptly. A frown took the place of that self-satisfied smile. "What are you talking about?"

"I can't keep up with your line of conquests," Dinah

murmured. "Dilly, is it? Or that girl in Costing with the big brown eyes?"

He looked taken aback. "Dilly?" he repeated. "You can't be serious."

"It's you who isn't serious, I suspect," Dinah bit out, her blue eyes glacial. "But Dilly may think you are." Dilly hoped he was, of course, but she wasn't telling him that. "You could hurt her, and she's just a baby; she's not used to men like you."

"Hurt Dilly?" he muttered, staring at her with icy glints in his eyes. "What on earth are you talking about?"

"Don't think I have any personal view on the matter," Dinah said through her teeth. "I don't care tuppence if you keep a whole harem. For all I know, you do. They don't call you the office sheik for nothing, I'm sure."

"The what?" he repeated, thunderstruck.

"Didn't you know? Oh, yes, that's your nickname down in the staff canteen. It keeps the gossips busy. 'Who is the sheik going to single out today?' they whisper as you walk past. Well, fine. Whatever turns you on, Mr. Randal. But if you have any heart at all, don't encourage Dilly, because she takes it all too seriously and what's just a game to you is a matter of life and death to her."

Greg Randal listened, his face now hard and taut, the strong jaw clenched as though to rein in the anger she could see in his darkened gray eyes.

"Got any more to say?" he asked when she stopped talking. "Or have you finished?"

Dinah threw caution to the winds, her temper racing

away with her. She was aware of having made a fool of herself in his arms and she turned on him in fury.

"No, I haven't finished. Dilly is just a kid. She's far too easily hurt, and I won't stand by and see you hurt her. Stay away from her. There are plenty of other girls around. You can take your pick."

"Why, thank you," he drawled sarcastically, the gray eyes filled with biting rage.

"Not at all," Dinah retorted. "I won't deny your sex appeal."

"You're too kind."

Her flush deepened and her blue eyes hated him. "Personally, I wouldn't have you at any price."

"Not even on a silver platter," he proffered as she paused to search for words.

"With an apple in your mouth," she agreed stingingly.

The dark flare of color in his face increased. "You've got a tongue like a scorpion," he flashed out. "As for my disastrous effect on Dilly, I'd advise you to mind your own business. What makes you think you know how to run other people's lives? You're hardly a wild success at running your own."

"I'm very happy with the way my life is run," Dinah threw back, wishing she meant it.

His mouth twisted. "You're proud of having destroyed a marriage, are you?"

"I didn't destroy anything!" She wouldn't have him saying things like that. They weren't true, and she wasn't going to let him accuse her without any grounds whatever.

"No, of course not," he smiled sardonically. "You're as innocent as a newborn baby."

"You drop dead," Dinah said in a hoarse, angry voice and went into her room and slammed the door violently in his face before he could stop her again.

She leaned on the door, fighting down a miserable desire to burst into tears. There was silence outside for a moment; then she heard him walk away very fast and slam his own door a moment later.

How am I supposed to get to sleep tonight? Dinah asked herself, but didn't get any answer. She didn't get much sleep, either. She tossed and turned in the bed, listening to the traffic whisk smoothly by in the street below. Dinah heard it so often in the night that it almost became a lullaby, the familiarity soothing.

The next morning she had her breakfast in her room. The waiter was cheerful, but Dinah felt like a corpse. She sipped her orange juice and drank her coffee black. The croissants she left untouched. She did not want anything to eat today. Her eyes were hot and dry from lack of sleep, and she was in a mood to be very difficult with any man she met, particularly Greg Randal.

The day he walked into his father's office she had taken one look and recognized the type. A flirt, she had thought, and promptly turned on the ice before he could start flirting with her, though it didn't seem to have done her any good in the end.

His own father had warned her not to take him seriously, not that she needed any warning, and in the intervening weeks she had heard through the office grapevine that his reputation as a lady-killer was well deserved. He had women lining up for his attention, she had been told, and she had believed it. She believed it even more now.

That technique of his was deadly. One kiss and she had been groggy. He hadn't learned that without practice. No wonder Dilly had looked like a sleepwalker the other night when Dinah had walked in and found her on the couch with him. No doubt he had been demonstrating his technique for Dilly, too, and it wouldn't take much to make Dilly's big eyes glaze over. She was a pushover, poor little Dilly.

Not me, though, Dinah told herself grimly. I'm not falling into his trap. His accusations about Andrew indicated what he thought of her. Perhaps he had imagined that a girl capable of breaking up a marriage was capable of enjoying a weekend fling in Paris, too, just on the side. He had been testing the ice last night, and for a brief moment of insanity Dinah had almost given way; but today the ice was going to be firmly back in place.

If Greg Randal thought for one second that he would get anywhere with her he was going to have to think again.

Chapter Six

There was a veiled enmity between them all that day. They had a series of meetings with people from the design team all the way up to the manager who would be taking over the Paris operation, and Greg was in a tense, businesslike mood from the start. Dinah watched him obliquely whenever she thought he wasn't aware of her, and she wouldn't have liked to argue with him in that mood. Everyone who came in contact with him steered clear of argument once they had picked up the glittering warning in his steely eyes.

The lazy charm was not much in evidence. Greg was taking no nonsense from anyone. He cut through confused explanations with curt phrases, making it clear that he wanted action, not words. He wasn't going to take any flack from anyone. It was almost miraculous, the way people who started out from entrenched positions hurriedly emerged to make compromises when Greg gave them that hard stare.

"He's the image of his father," the Paris manager told her over lunch. "Sir Gee all over again." He was half admiring, half aghast. "I didn't think there could be two of them. I had the idea Greg was a much easier type. Boy, was I wrong."

"You were," Dinah agreed dryly, inspecting her langoustine in mayonnaise without enthusiasm. She did not much care for shellfish. And she didn't even want to eat today to begin with.

The Frenchman gave her an admiring stare. "He knows how to pick a secretary," he told her. Dinah smiled politely. She had met Pierre Roland before; he had spent a year working in London some time back. Dinah had been a far more junior member of the staff then, but she had met him once or twice and had fended off his halfhearted attempts to make dates with her. He was an easygoing man. He had accepted her refusals without taking offense, which made him someone she rather liked. It made life much easier if men took that attitude.

Dinah had often pondered on the way some men seemed to take it as a personal offense if you showed no sign of responding to their overtures. Why should they imagine they only had to ask to receive? Relationships between the sexes were always complicated, but if a man couldn't take no for an answer they could become very difficult.

"How long will you be in Paris?" Pierre asked, and she told him that they were there for just two days.

"If you have any free time I'd be glad to show you

something of Paris," he offered without pushing the point.

Dinah liked that. He was leaving her a way out if she chose to take it. Hesitating, she caught Greg's eye from the far end of the table. There was dark impatience in his stare. Dinah gave the other man a warmer smile than she would have done normally and answered, "Thank you, I'd like that."

He looked surprised but delighted. "My pleasure," he murmured. "What about tonight?"

"Lovely," Dinah said. It would get her out of spending another evening with Greg Randal, anyway, and she knew she could handle Pierre Roland. He had very good manners and he wouldn't make the evening uncomfortable for her. At least there were some gentlemen left in the world, Dinah thought to herself as she let her eyes glance from Pierre to Greg.

"Where would you like to go?" he asked. "Dinner? The opera? The theater?"

Dinah's French was not up to the theater. She spoke it to a point, the point where she found herself stammering through complicated sentences in which she lost her way. Simple phrases were what she stuck to—but they wouldn't help her at the theater.

"The opera would be nice," she said, and Pierre inclined his smooth dark head.

"Fine." His English was very good, although he spoke it with a faint transatlantic drawl. He had learned his English in the States and he was sometimes hard to understand when his rapid-fire French delivery got wrapped up in colloquial Americanisms. "They're doing Offenbach," he told her. "They used to do nothing but operetta, you know, but they're branching out now and trying other stuff. Tonight, though, it's good old Offenbach."

"I like operetta myself," Dinah told him.

He smiled. "The ladies usually do," he agreed.

"But not you?"

"I like Wagner," he murmured, and Dinah made a face.

"Too heavy for me."

"Exciting, though, and when it's well done it's superb musically." Pierre Roland watched the wine waiter fill her glass. "You like French wine?"

"Very much," Dinah said, although she rarely drank very much of it. A glass or two occasionally was pleasant, but it somehow seemed to send her almost directly to sleep.

"I'll pick you up at your hotel at seven," Pierre told her. "We'll have supper after the opera, shall we?"

"I'd enjoy that," Dinah frowned. "Should I wear evening dress, do you think?"

Pierre nodded. "People do. It makes it more of an occasion, you know." He gave her a concerned glance. "Do you have evening dress with you?"

"Oh, yes," Dinah said casually, making a mental note to rush out and buy herself something to wear that afternoon.

Greg kept her busy, but around four thirty she got a chance to slip off alone. She caught a taxi outside the hotel and shot off to the Galeries Lafayette, where she wandered around the boutiques inside the store until she found a dress she liked. It cost far more than she would normally have paid for a dress. She had to think more than twice before she settled on it, but she felt restless and defiant. She felt like doing something crazy.

Living alone in London, Dinah had learned to exist on a tight budget. She was very careful with her money. Dilly might blow a week's income on a dress when the mood took her, but Dinah was more concerned with paying the rent, the electricity bill and the telephone bill. She had much more of a sense of responsibility. When they came in each quarter Dilly would look pink and sheepish before she confessed she hadn't quite got enough for her own share of the expenses. Jennifer and Dinah would glance at each other and sigh, "Oh, Dilly." They were never surprised. Dilly had no idea of how to handle money and they always expected her confession. It would astonish them far more if Dilly promptly paid up what she owed. Every quarter they made sure the bills were paid, and Dilly's share came in bit by bit as she remembered to pay them. It wasn't fair, but Dinah and Jennifer felt sorry for Dilly.

Arriving back at the hotel, she found Greg in the cocktail bar with a glass of Pernod and black currant in front of him. He looked up as she tried to slip past the entrance. Dinah couldn't quite pretend she hadn't noticed the lean finger crooked in her direction.

"Oh, hello," she said coolly, meeting his eyes as she walked toward him.

"And where have you been?" He slid that narrowed gaze down to the large bag she was carrying.

"Shopping," she said, in what she hoped was a lively voice. "You didn't need me, did you?"

"I did," he said, clipping the words out as if biting them off with his teeth.

"Sorry," Dinah murmured. She half turned to go,

but Greg's hand shot out to fix around her wrist like an iron bracelet.

"Sit down," he said, in a tone which did not admit the possibility of a refusal.

Dinah sat. Greg released her and she pointedly nursed her wrist, looking in an accusing way at the thin red mark he had left.

The waiter swam up to wait for orders. Greg looked at his own glass. "The same for the lady," he said.

"What is it?" Dinah asked, looking at the drink without much enthuasiasm.

"Pernod and black currant," Greg told her.

It sounded vile. "I've never tasted Pernod," Dinah admitted, still gently rubbing her wrist. She felt as if it might never be the same again. Greg's fingers had cut off her blood supply and now her veins were tingling as it returned.

Ignoring her comment, Greg asked, "What was that at lunch about you and Roland?"

"He's taking me to the opera," Dinah said as the waiter came back with her drink.

"He's what?" Greg's retort came like a gunshot, making her jump.

She picked up her glass and sipped, making a surprised face. "Quite nice; I like it."

Greg was not put off. "Have you met him before?" he wanted to know, and Dinah nodded as she sipped again. Sweet but very pleasant, she decided.

"How well do you know him?"

"He worked in London for a while," Dinah reminded him. "I met him then. I worked with him for months; it was before I worked for your father."

"I've made arrangements for this evening," Greg

said moodily, staring at her. "Why didn't you ask me before accepting Roland's invitation?"

Dinah said she was sorry, she hadn't thought of it. "I suppose I assumed I was free," she added in dulcet calm.

"Don't make assumptions again," Greg informed her with icy dislike.

"I'll try not to," Dinah promised, finishing her drink and standing up. The mixture of aniseed and black currant might taste innocuous, but it was stronger than it wanted you to think. It had quite an afterkick. She smiled sunnily at Greg as she moved away. That had been easier than she had anticipated.

She took some time in getting ready. Her dress was white, a clinging silk concoction which followed the outline of her curved body with faithful simplicity down to her feet. The folds had a classical Grecian look, the material so beautifully cut that it needed someone with a good figure to wear it. Slit at the sides, it was easy to wear, the silk sliding back as she walked to reveal her long, slim legs to the knee.

Dinah wound her blond hair into a high-piled chignon, the style exposing her bare nape. She had a faint qualm about the rather low neckline as she regarded herself in the mirror. Her pale shoulders and the beginnings of her high breasts did look rather exposed to her, but Pierre Roland's good manners were unlikely to slip, she decided. She could manage him.

The telephone rang. It was reception. Pierre had arrived and was waiting for her in the cocktail lounge, she was told. "I won't be a moment," promised Dinah. She gave herself a last thoughtful stare and then went down.

She had not expected to find Greg with Pierre. They were seated at one of the tables with drinks in front of them, and as Dinah sailed into the room they both looked up.

Pierre's dark eyes sparked in Gallic appreciation as he rose. Dinah concentrated on him, smiling, but it was Greg's reaction she was most aware of. He took a moment to recover from his apparent stupefaction and only got up as she reached the table.

Pierre took her hand and kissed it reverently. "You are very lovely," he told her in a deep and thrilling voice.

Dinah suppressed a desire to laugh. Somehow his admiration seemed theatrical. She sat down and casually glanced at Greg.

He was still standing, his face harsh, and he was staring at her with narrowed, leaping gray eyes. When he did sink back into his place he picked up his glass of whiskey and swallowed it as though he were dying of thirst.

"What will you have to drink, Dinah?" asked Pierre, and she told him she would have white wine. She glanced through her lashes at Greg, who was considering his empty glass with expressionless interest.

Both men were in evening dress. Pierre was a tall, slim man who looked very good in it, but Greg looked breathtaking. He always did. That lean, powerful body imposed itself on the elegant formality of the dark material, making her far too aware of his sexual potency. She struggled to look as cool as she wanted him to think she was, but her throat had begun to pulse with a fever she had never felt before, and she swallowed as she looked away.

110

"Do you like opera, Greg?" Pierre asked, politely bringing Greg into the conversation.

Greg nodded without looking up. Pierre began to talk about his favorite music, and the other two listened with as much intent absorption as though he were fascinating them.

"Where are you off to tonight?" Pierre inquired after a while.

Greg said brusquely, "I'm dining out."

Pierre laughed, his brown skin wrinkling with teasing amusement. "And is she pretty?"

"What?" Greg looked up then, his black brows a menacing bar across his forehead.

Pierre looked alarmed. He was a man who believed in making his boss happy. He didn't want to offend Sir Gee's son and heir.

Dinah intervened smoothly. "I think things are going very smoothly now, don't you, Pierre? The design team seem to be coming to a conclusion at last."

"Oh, yes," he said eagerly, grateful for the change of subject. "We're finally seeing things happen. Thanks to you, Greg," he added, giving Greg a soothing little smile.

Greg did not look around. He looked like a man who might suddenly start breaking things. Pierre automatically invited him to have another drink, hurriedly summoning the waiter. Greg asked for a whiskey, got it, and drank it in two swallows while Pierre watched him in curious surprise and Dinah stared intently into her own glass.

"Good night," Greg muttered through his teeth, getting up. He was gone before Pierre could say anything else. Pierre looked glumly at Dinah.

"He is in a bad mood."

"Isn't he?" Dinah said, brittle gaiety in her voice. She drank her wine, and Pierre escorted her out of the hotel.

Until now she had only seen the Paris opera house from the outside. The architecture was classical and ornate, the green dome which rose above the building decorated with a great gilded centerpiece on which some dancing figures were perched. The Place de l'Opéra was lit by dusky street lamps of the Second Empire period, their Victorian flavor oddly matching the Gothic taste of the opera house itself.

Traffic swirled around the building in a noisy flood, but inside all was civilized, calm and luxurious. Dinah made her way up the red-carpeted stairs with Pierre and heard the orchestra tuning up.

"A magical moment," Pierre whispered, as they took their seats and looked toward the crimson curtains.

"I love it when the curtain opens," Dinah murmured back, smiling at him. At that moment the house lights went down and the audience settled back into their seats with a low, anticipatory murmur as the overture began.

Dinah tried to concentrate on the music, but her unruly mind kept wandering off toward forbidden subjects. She dragged it back from its contemplation of Greg Randal and insisted that it must stay on the matter in hand. Once the curtains had opened to warm applause it was easier. She watched and listened, her thoughts wandering less when the stage could hold them fixed.

During the interval they went out to the bar to have a

drink. Dinah was thirsty. The opera house was crowded and very overheated. She drank lemonade while Pierre had a glass of white wine. The noise rose around them, French voices rapid and excited in discussion of what they had just seen. Most of the audience in the dress circle wore evening dress. Many of them wore jewels, too, and the bar was packed with elegant people who talked with expert enthusiasm about music. Dinah couldn't understand half of what was said around her, but she found it fun to listen and try to pick out the odd phrase.

"You're enjoying it?" Pierre spoke close to her. He had been crushed up next to her by the sheer press of bodies in the tiny bar.

"Very much. You?"

"I always do," he said. "I come regularly."

"You like music, obviously."

"Any music," he agreed, grinning. "Even jazz."

"I love jazz," Dinah said. "Traditional, anyway."

They talked about that for a while until the bell went and the bar emptied as everyone trooped back to their seats.

When they left the opera they took a taxi to a small French restaurant on the Left Bank, crossing the dark Seine by the Pont de la Concorde. It was strange to emerge from the narrow, busy streets behind the Place de la Concorde and find oneself in that echoing open space. Dinah stared out the taxi window as they drove through the swerving traffic.

"Paris is beautiful," she murmured, and Pierre looked pleased but hardly surprised. Every Frenchman expects to hear that.

"London is very interesting," he complimented her in the voice of one struggling to be just. "I enjoyed my stay there."

"But you were glad to get back," Dinah teased, and he smiled sideways at her, his dark eyes amused.

"I am afraid so; Paris is a city for living in, you know? The street cafés, the public buildings, the boulevards—only the French know how to live in a city. London is harder to get to know, I found. You cannot sit down in a street bar and watch the girls and talk to strangers, as you can in Paris. It is not accepted in the same way. You can do almost anything here, Dinah. At night Paris is still alive, awake, but by midnight London is asleep for the night."

Dinah looked around as they drove along the Boulevard Saint Michel. She could see what he meant. It was very late, but the pavements were crowded with young people and the roads were jammed with noisy traffic. Paris was very much awake and enjoying itself.

They found a candlelit table and ate a leisurely meal while a small jazz band performed in a corner. Some of the customers wore evening dress, while others wore jeans. Nobody seemed to care which—the waiters treated all their customers alike, their attitude to the food they served that of high priests, reverential and enthusiastic.

It was two in the morning before Pierre dropped Dinah at the hotel. She was very sleepy, but she had had a fantastic evening and she felt very good as she stumbled out of the lift on her floor.

The lock on her door was as recalcitrant as ever. She fumbled with it, yawning.

Another door flew open a few feet away. Dinah glanced around, suppressing another yawn, and met dangerous gray eyes.

"Where the devil have you been?"

He was beside her like a streak of lightning, and Dinah came awake with a rush.

"Oh, hello," she said, leaning against the door because her legs had just turned to rubber.

The door swung inward at the pressure and she stumbled with it, giving a little yelp of surprise.

Greg said something explosive under his breath. "You're drunk," he accused, grabbing her around the waist to support her.

Dinah slapped down his hands, drawing herself up with dignity and hauteur. "I most certainly am not."

"What have you been doing until this hour?" he demanded, looking into her sleepy blue eyes with harsh impatience. "Where have you been until now?"

"We had supper," Dinah said, defending her whereabouts. Greg was in a short toweling robe, his long legs bare and dark beneath the white material. Dinah found her eyes dwelling on the strong bare throat visible between the lapels. She hurriedly looked away.

"Supper," he said, as though the word made no sense at all. He was staring at her fixedly.

"Supper," Dinah repeated patiently. "Very good, too. Pierre knows his restaurants. We had the most fantastic meal I've ever tasted, five courses of it. I don't know how I'll sleep tonight."

"Wound up, are you?" Greg asked nastily. "It must have been a good evening."

She didn't like the way he said that. She didn't think he was talking about the effect of the food. He somehow managed to look as if she had behaved badly, as if he were accusing her of something.

"Did you enjoy yourself," she inquired with sweet courtesy.

"Oh, I had a great time," Greg muttered.

"Good." Dinah backed away. "Good night, then," she told him, closing the door, half afraid he might block it with his tall, powerful body.

He went without answering, and she shut the door completely and leaned on it, breathing fast. Her head was going around in circles, and it wasn't just the effect of the wine she had drunk with her supper. Greg Randal was much headier. When he had been staring at her just now she had felt her veins pulsing with strange heat, her skin prickling with awareness and restless fever.

Why couldn't he have been fast asleep? He hadn't looked very sleepy. He had looked as if he had been wide awake for hours. She stripped off her dress and underclothes and took a shower, the warm water sluicing down her back and making her skin tingle.

As she got into bed she told herself she was not going to dwell on thoughts of Greg Randal. The room was silent and shadowy, a thin streak of light making an entrance through the curtains to flick around the room with fugitive restlessness.

Sleep descended before she saw it coming. When she woke up her telephone was shrilling, and she started out of a deep dream to grope across the bedside table to silence it. "What?" she mumbled into the receiver, still dazed.

"It is nine o'clock," said a curt voice. "Are you working today?"

Dinah put a hand to her throbbing head. "Yes. I overslept. Sorry."

"Have you had breakfast?"

She shuddered. "I don't want any." She couldn't eat a single thing. The idea made her ill.

Greg laughed unpleasantly. "Morning after the night before, is it? I'm not surprised."

"I've got a headache, that's all," Dinah retorted, adding with a spurt of irritation, "I'm not having a hangover. I was not drunk."

"Oh, no, of course not," he drawled, and she made a face at her receiver. "I'm starting the first meeting in a quarter of an hour. Get down here as soon as you can." The phone slammed down, and she gave a groan as her ear reverberated with the sound.

Another shower woke her up a little. She dressed in a black shirt and a pleated white skirt, belted it tightly around her slim waist, and made her way downstairs. They were still serving breakfast. Dinah had some black coffee, sipping it without much enthusiasm.

When she slipped into the conference room which Greg had hired for the day heads turned to observe her with amused curiosity. Greg was the only one who didn't look around. He went on talking in a crisp, cool voice, and after a few seconds the men all turned back to watch him.

Peering at her across the table, Pierre gave her a ghost of a wink. She smiled wanly at him. Did he feel as bad as she did? Maybe he was used to eating huge meals at night. Maybe it didn't bother his digestion. It wasn't the wine she had drunk, she knew. It was the food she had eaten which was the cause of her dullness this morning. Normally Dinah nibbled a lettuce leaf or had some toast in the evening. Five-course meals were not her normal diet, especially when the food was so rich and coated in sauces made of cream, butter and eggs. French people must have cast-iron digestions, she decided.

The morning dragged past. Dinah skipped lunch. She couldn't have eaten a thing. French food was not on her mind. She went out for a stroll instead, enjoying the feel of the Paris sunshine on her skin as she wandered along the great open boulevard. Famous French names caught her eye in every shop. She would have liked to buy herself something with one of those world-renowned labels on it, but she had already spent too much on her dress.

When she got back to the conference room she was late again. Greg menaced her with a tight smile. "How kind of you to join us," he said sarcastically.

"Sorry," she mumbled, feeling, rather than seeing, the grins the other men wore. This just wasn't her day. They were discussing the marketing problems of the new French operation. Dinah opened the file and pretended to flick through it, keeping her head down. The most she could hope for was that she would avoid attracting Greg Randal's attention for the next few hours.

The meeting broke up with handshakes and smiles. Dinah slid discreetly out of the room and got back to her own room safely and without trouble. Her bed looked very inviting. She lay down on it and closed her eyes. The telephone went.

"Yes?" She knew who it was before he spoke.

"I hope you remembered what I said."

"What was that?" she asked warily, not pretending that she didn't know who it was because there was no point. She would recognize that deep, curt voice anywhere.

"I told you to keep this evening free."

"Oh," she said, desperately trying to think of an excuse. "Well, actually, I'm rather tired."

"Too bad," Greg said. "I'll see you in the bar at seven."

The phone went dead, and she glared at it before replacing her receiver. She had often wondered how Lady Randal kept her happy smile married to Sir Gee, and now she wondered what sort of stupid female would ever marry Greg Randal. He might be a sexy man with unmistakable charisma, but he was also, on occasion, maddening and infuriating.

I wouldn't have him at any price, Dinah told herself as she got dressed. She had little choice of what to wear. Black or white? She shrugged. White it would have to be—she had the feeling Greg would look sideways at her if she came down wearing anything else. He would be pretty sure she had chosen to play for safety. The white dress might be stunning, but it did not err on the side of safety. She had been sure Pierre would behave himself if she wore it, but she felt no such confidence about Greg Randal.

They dined at the hotel, and Dinah was relieved about that. She could always make an excuse and disappear upstairs if she got too bothered.

And she was bothered; that was the trouble. Greg Randal bothered her. She had stopped pretending to herself that he didn't. Every time he looked at her she felt electricity tingle along her veins. Every time he spoke her blood beat loudly in her ears. Every time she was with him she felt this unbelievable change come over her. It was very hard to have a polite conversation with someone when he had such a devastating effect on you. She found it hard to keep her mind on what he said. Her own feelings were too engrossing. From the grim way he kept looking at her she knew that he had noticed her abstraction.

"Sorry to be so boring," he snarled at one point, giving her the sort of look which is like a knife between the shoulder blades. "Maybe some black coffee will wake you up."

She apologized, flushing, but it didn't soften the harsh contours of his face. They had their coffee in silence. He made no attempt to talk to her.

Only as they rose to go did he ask, "What time is our flight tomorrow?"

"Nine thirty," she said, rustling as she walked at his side, the slit skirt smoothly sliding back to give glimpses of her calf.

He angrily struck the lift button and the doors opened. Following her inside, he said, "Well, we've achieved what we came for, I suppose. It should all go ahead quite nicely now."

"Your father will be delighted."

"He is," Greg said, his mouth twisting. "I talked to him on the phone before dinner."

"How's your grandmother?"

"Demanding to be allowed out of bed and giving everyone a bad time," he said, smiling with real warmth for the first time that evening. "So I guess you could say 'no change,'" he mused.

"She's marvelous," Dinah said, smiling back at him.

He walked out of the lift beside her, his long strides effortlessly keeping pace. Pausing at her door, Dinah said with dry-mouthed nervousness, "Well, good night. Thanks for the dinner. I enjoyed it very much."

He put a hand flat on the wall, leaning over her, his wide shoulders relaxed beneath the evening suit. "That dress could drive a man insane," he whispered tormentingly, smiling into her eyes.

Dinah backed away, trembling. Oh, no, she thought, feeling the flare of excitement running through her veins. All she had to do was keep him at arm's length for another few moments and the dangerous cliff edge of passion would be safely past. She had managed to keep the temperature low all through dinner. She was not going to let it shoot upward now.

"Good night," she repeated, sliding backward into her room, her eyes warily fixed on him.

"If you can flirt with Pierre Roland you can flirt with me," Greg said, his smile going and a glittering anger coming into his eyes.

"I didn't flirt with Pierre, and I'm not going to flirt with you, either," Dinah assured him in what she very much hoped he would take for a cool, distant voice.

"No?" Greg advanced menacingly.

"No," Dinah said, retreating. ―

He was inside her room before she had realized the folly of going backward without closing the door between them.

"You're a cold-blooded little tease," he accused, coming on at a faster pace until she was within reach. His hand shot out to encircle her waist, and she

121

struggled to push it away, her blue eyes angry and disturbed.

"I don't know what sort of impression you've got of me," she began, and Greg laughed between his teeth, his hard mouth twisting into derisive contempt.

"No?"

She eyed him with rage. "I'm not the sort of girl you seem to think I am."

"I know what sort of girl you are—the sort who cheerfully breaks up a marriage and then goes off for the evening with a Frenchman she barely knows and stays out until the early hours of the morning with him. The sort of girl who wears a dress which shrieks sex appeal and then tries to pretend she didn't mean it." Greg was talking very fast, his voice shaking with temper. "Well, when you beckon with one hand and try to push a man away with the other, you'd better expect trouble, lady." His eyes flashed down over her, and she burned with a strange mixture of excitement and fear at his expression. "And tonight, trouble is what you're going to get," he promised in a low, silky voice which sent shivers down her spine.

Her free hand groped around desperately and knocked the lamp off the table behind her. Greg looked around in startled surprise. Dinah spun free from him and rushed over to the bathroom. Before he had realized what she meant to do she had locked herself inside.

For a few seconds she stood there, listening, her heartbeat almost deafening her. She heard movements; then the door of her room slammed violently. Dinah didn't trust him. She waited for ten minutes before she warily peered out into the room. It was empty. She shot the bolt with trembling hands and stood there, her eyes closed. That was close, she thought.

It was very late before she got to sleep that night. She was so tired that she was almost hallucinating, but she could not shut off her mind. She kept remembering that look Greg had given her, the dangerous mixture of rage and desire it had held. It haunted her sleep, too. She woke up in the morning, weary and stiff, with memories of dreams which she would prefer to forget, and at last she had to admit to herself that she was helplessly, hopelessly in love with Greg Randal.

Her emotions had been so tangled and she had resisted admitting them for so long that the feeling had grown deeper and deeper before she was ready to face it. She faced it now, in the pale light of a Paris dawn, listening to the distant echo of the traffic making its way through the streets below. Why did she have to fall in love with him? Why didn't she keep the promise she'd made to herself, and not fall into his trap? How could she let herself love a man like Greg Randal? All these questions boggled her mind.

It was a useless waste of feeling. Greg Randal might want her, but he was not the marrying kind. His own father had warned her as much. She could see it for herself. He was in his thirties, but he had never come anywhere near marrying, and no doubt when he did he would choose the girl his mother planned as his wife. Greg, like Sir Gee, was a strong family man and he adored his mother. He would do what the family expected him to do.

If he guessed how Dinah felt about him, though, he wouldn't hesitate about trying to talk her into bed. The way he had been behaving in Paris made that painfully clear. Greg Randal was a typical opportunistic male. Once he realized he could turn her on, he would try to do so, using every weapon he possessed—and Greg Randal had any number of sexual weapons. He could make a pulse miss whenever he smiled sideways or spoke in that husky voice.

Dinah shivered, curling up into a miserable ball in the bed. She would despise herself if she let Greg sweet-talk her into bed. Falling in love had made her come fiercely, painfully alive. She should have known that her strange alternation of highs and lows, her elations and depressions lately, had come from being in love. The beginning of love might be more high than low, but if she allowed herself to slide into an affair with Greg, knowing he would end it some day, she would be left with a bitter residue of self-contempt and pain.

"No," she said aloud, her voice breaking. Tears burned behind her eyes. She would ride it out somehow. She would force it out of sight and out of mind. Love, like a plant, needs oxygen before it can grow. Dinah meant to stifle her love before it grew any deeper.

Chapter Seven

The returning flight to London was as silent as the flight to Paris had been. Dinah and Greg sat side by side and ignored each other totally. When the stewardess brought them coffee, giving Greg an inviting little smile, Dinah felt like baring her teeth at the girl, but she forced a smile herself as she accepted her tray. Greg went one better. He said something to the stewardess which made her blush and flutter her false lashes before she moved away. Dinah pretended she hadn't noticed. If he wanted to flirt with air hostesses that was up to him, and she didn't care.

She had known he was a flirt the minute she set eyes on him; it should have been satisfying to be proved right. It wasn't.

They shared a taxi into London, driving along the barren wastelands of the motorway from Heathrow. Greg buried himself in the newspaper he had been reading with relentless determination ever since they left France. Dinah stared out the window, aching to see the shabby hinterland of London appear.

He gave her a curt nod when the taxi stopped outside her flat. The taxi driver helped her to the door with her suitcase; Greg stayed behind his newspaper. "Lovely man, isn't he?" the driver said sarcastically. "A real gentleman."

"Drop him into the Thames as you go by," Dinah said with biting relish as she let herself into the house.

The flat was empty. She put down her suitcase and looked around with depressed ruefulness. It looked smaller, shabbier and even less homelike than usual. Dilly had left a bowl of half-eaten cereal on the table. Jennifer's row of drying tights was visible in the bathroom.

"Home, sweet home," Dinah muttered, wondering where to start to make the room look less like a refugee center.

She ate some scraps of salad for lunch. That was all she could find in the kitchen: a little lettuce, a tomato and some sticks of celery. It didn't matter; she wasn't hungry.

When she had unpacked, she looked at the clock and decided to try to see Judy's parents. Dinah had been to their house several times. They had not been very friendly but at least they did know her by sight.

The blue sky was clouding over as she arrived at their suburban home. She saw a few large spots of rain spreading behind her on the garden path and huddled under the porch. The door opened and Judy's mother stared at her, her face stiffening.

"Remember me?" Dinah asked hopefully, with a smile.

"Yes," the woman said without one.

Dinah was surprised and taken aback by that tone, by the cold face she saw. "I wonder if I could talk to you?" she asked in an uncertain voice.

"What about?" She wasn't being given any encouragement. Judy's mother looked at her with unhidden dislike.

"Judy," Dinah said rather nervously. "I'm worried. . . ."

"So you should be!"

"What?" Dinah stared, even more dismayed by the icy retort. Of course, it was clear that Mrs. Rogers was upset over her daughter's marital problems, but it was hardly Dinah's fault that Judy had run off to another man.

"You ought to be ashamed," Mrs. Rogers informed her in a louder and angrier voice, the flush growing on her cheeks. She was a short, stout woman with a naturally high color, but she was beginning to look very red in the face now.

"Me?" Dinah repeated, unable to believe her ears.

"Yes, you, coming between a man and his wife."

Dinah's lips parted on a soundless gasp. "I haven't done anything of the kind. What are you talking about?"

"You and Andrew," Mrs. Rogers accused. "They would have been happy if it hadn't been for you."

"Me?" Dinah was reduced to repeating it again, her voice stunned. She couldn't believe this was happening. When Greg Randal accused her of interfering between Andrew and his wife she had dismissed his suspicions without taking any notice of them because she had known the truth. Didn't Judy's mother know about the other man, either? Had Judy lied to her parents?

"I don't know how you have the nerve to come here," Mrs. Rogers told her angrily.

"Mrs. Rogers, I don't know where you got your information from, but you're wrong about me and Andrew," Dinah said, getting angry herself suddenly. She was not going to have the whole world believing that she had been instrumental in wrecking a marriage. Andrew's pride was not as important as her own good name.

The woman snorted, putting her hands on her hips and glaring at Dinah. "Oh, am I? My daughter tells me lies, does she?"

"If she told you that, then I'm afraid she does," Dinah said unhappily. "It is Judy who is in love with someone else, not Andrew."

"Rubbish," said Mrs. Rogers. "Oh, she told Andrew that. I know she did. I said she was being stupid for making up a story like that. It won't bring him back. She had some crazy idea it might make him jealous and make him want her again—"

"You mean it isn't true?" Dinah interrupted, staring at her with enormous, astonished eyes.

"Of course not. Judy loves her husband." Mrs. Rogers stared at Dinah. "You've made my daughter very unhappy, miss. I hope that satisfies you."

"It doesn't satisfy me," Dinah said, trembling with consternation and distress. "I had no idea. You're wrong—both you and Judy. There's absolutely nothing like that between me and Andrew. He's more like a brother to me. He always has been. We've known each other all our lives. I *couldn't* feel romantic about him. I'd be more likely to feel romantic about the milkman."

Mrs. Rogers backed up, her mouth open. After a long silence she said, "You'd better come in. Maybe this whole mess can be straightened out."

"Thank you," Dinah said, advancing as the drumming of the rain increased behind her. The hall door shut and Dinah followed Mrs. Rogers into the sitting room, where a ginger cat sat purring by an electric fire. The room was overheated, but Dinah ignored that, taking the chair Mrs. Rogers indicated.

"Why have you come?" Judy's mother asked, sitting down opposite her.

"To try to talk to Judy," Dinah said. "Andrew's so unhappy over all this. He believed her. About the other man, I mean. He *is* miserable, Mrs. Rogers."

"Always running off to you, though, isn't he?" The other woman might believe Dinah's insistence that she was not in love with Andrew, but there was still accusation in her eyes. "How do you think that looked to my Judy? Every time they had a little quarrel, off he would rush to you. What was she to think?"

"It never occurred to me," Dinah murmured, frowning.

"Look at it from her point of view," Mrs. Rogers said, shifting in her chair.

Dinah *was* looking at it from Judy's point of view and feeling rather stupid. "I should have realized," she muttered.

"You should." Mrs. Rogers was not sparing her, her voice still stiff with anger. "It got worse and worse. The more they quarreled, the more Andrew seemed to prefer you."

That was true, no doubt. Andrew did not like quarrels. He fled them like the plague. As Dinah had often reflected, his own home background had been so calm and contented that he had not been prepared for the more volatile moods of his young wife. Dinah looked back over the past year and saw it all very differently. Far from easing the situation by giving Andrew tea and sympathy, she had been making it all more troubled and more explosive. She should have left Andrew to cope with his wife on his own. A marriage was a private affair. She shouldn't have allowed him to drag her into it.

She sighed. "Do you think Judy will see me? I must talk to her, get her to understand how wrong she has been."

Mrs. Rogers hesitated. "I don't know, I'm sure."

"Please," Dinah begged. "For Judy's sake, I must explain things to her myself."

Mrs. Rogers gave her the address of the flat to which Judy had moved. "She won't be very pleased to see you, mind," she warned as Dinah left.

The rain was still pouring down. Dinah made a face at it as she halted on the little porch. "No, I realize that," she said, before she made a run for it. She got a bus at the corner of the road. Her blond hair was saturated and her jacket was clinging damply to her back as she sank into the seat.

How stupid can you be? she asked herself, staring out at the rain-washed streets as the bus lumbered through them. Why didn't it ever dawn on me? Of course, I only heard Andrew's side of it all. He had no idea, obviously. It hadn't even crossed his mind. Andrew would be stricken with embarrassed dismay if he found out. Dinah knew he had never had a shred of romantic interest in her, any more than she had had in him.

She got off the bus at a stop close to Judy's flat and hurried along the road, getting wetter than ever. She swallowed her trepidation and knocked. There was a light in the window, and after a pause Judy opened the door and looked at her with biting fury before she tried to shut it again.

"I've got to talk to you," Dinah insisted, putting her foot in the door and almost getting it crushed.

"Go away," hissed Judy through the crack.

"It isn't true," Dinah said. "Andrew and I just aren't that way about each other. We never were. I had no idea you thought such stupid things."

"Will you go away, or do I have to call the police?" Judy burst out in a shaking voice, her eyes blazing.

"It isn't true," Dinah said again. "I wouldn't have Andrew if you handed him to me on a plate. He wouldn't have me, either. He's more like a brother and certainly not a lover."

She thought she saw a faint uncertainty in Judy's face and pressed her advantage.

"Andrew doesn't turn me on. I don't fancy him."

Judy opened the door another inch. "He fancies you, though," she muttered, her lip trembling.

"Never," Dinah said loudly. "Not in a million years. Do you think I wouldn't know? You can't miss it when a man fancies you. Now, can you?"

Judy slowly swung the door open. "Are you sure?"

"Certain," Dinah said, smiling.

"Then why does he keep running off to see you?" Judy stood in her path, her color coming and going.

"He's an idiot," Dinah said gently. "Look, if I were his sister, would you be surprised or angry if he confided in me?"

"Yes," Judy said involuntarily and gave a weak little groan of laughter. "Probably," she added.

Dinah assessed her thoughtfully. Yes, she realized. Judy had been honest there. She was the jealous type. It stood out a mile. She wouldn't stand for sharing Andrew with anybody, even a sister. Why on earth hadn't she realized that before?

"He's mine," Judy said on a fierce note, reddening a second later. She met Dinah's glance with defiance. "That's how I feel," she said, not backing down.

"You've never told him you're jealous of me, have you?" Dinah asked. "Look, can I come in, or are we going to conduct the rest of this conversation on the step? Because if so I ought to tell you that the lady in the next flat is listening through her lace curtains. And, besides, I'm soaking wet."

Judy looked around, and the lace curtain suddenly flapped as the shape behind it vanished.

"Come in," Judy said, marching away.

Her flat was smaller and even less homelike than Dinah's. It must be a depressing place to sit and be unhappy in, Dinah thought, looking around the tiny room.

"Clear a space," Judy offered gruffly. "Like some coffee?"

"Please," Dinah said, removing a pile of magazines from a chair and sitting down. Judy went over to the curtained-off kitchenette and filled the kettle. "Instant, I'm afraid."

"That's fine," Dinah said cheerfully.

When Judy came back with the steaming cups they sat and looked at each other across a barbed-wire silence.

"What are we going to do?" Dinah asked.

"*We?*" asked Judy coldly.

"I'm involved, too," Dinah pointed out. "Look, if you're wise you won't tell Andrew what you suspected. He wouldn't like it."

"Isn't that too bad?" Judy dropped lumps of sugar into her coffee and handed Dinah the bowl. "Sugar?" she asked, as though inviting Dinah to take poison.

Dinah shook her head. "It's up to you," she began again, and Judy cut in venomously to say, "It is, isn't it?"

Flushing, Dinah grimaced. "Yes, I get the point. I've interfered enough."

"You said it," Judy informed her.

"I honestly had no idea."

Judy studied her with acute dislike. "What difference does that make? If you hadn't been there, Andrew and I would never have quarreled in the first place."

You can't argue with jealousy, Dinah realized. Judy was never going to like her much. The best she could hope for was that she would stop hating her enough to want to poison her coffee.

"You are going to see him, though? You can't let your marriage break up over nothing."

Judy put down her cup undrunk. "That's my business," she said. Then she gave a long sigh. "Oh, I appreciate your coming to see me. I'm glad you told me the truth."

"And you believe me?"

"I suppose so," Judy said without total faith.

Dinah hesitated, her color deepening. "Because it's not only that I don't love Andrew, you see. There's someone else."

Judy sat up. "Oh."

Dinah had not wanted to say that, but she had seen that Judy needed further proof. "I'm in the same boat as Andrew," she murmured, her eyes on her coffee. "The guy I love thinks the same as you. He got the impression I was having an affair with Andrew, too. I should have realized it looked like that, but it never even entered my head. I've looked on Andy as a brother for so long that I assumed everyone else thought like that, too. I see I was wrong. More wrong than I'd ever imagined."

Judy watched her, frowning. "Have you told him the truth? Your guy, I mean."

Dinah made a little face. "It wouldn't make any difference. He isn't in love with me. I shan't bother. But you and Andy—that matters. You must make up your quarrel. Poor Andy is going round the bend. He looks terrible. He isn't sleeping, you know. He looks very ill."

"Does he?" Judy sat forward, her voice husky. "Does he, really?"

It was the final breakthrough. Dinah stayed for another half hour, painting for Judy a pathetic picture of Andy at the end of his tether, going out of his mind, unable to eat and ready to go on his knees at the first word from Judy.

When she left she felt that for the first time she had come close to being friendly with Andrew's wife. It was a fragile friendship which might snap if too much weight was placed on it, though. In the future, Dinah was going to have to be very wary in her relationship with Andrew. She was going to have to keep him at a distance now. Andrew must learn to cope with his marriage without rushing off to Dinah for help. She wouldn't help him anymore—he'd have to work it out with Judy.

Had Judy learned anything from it? Dinah couldn't be sure of that. Judy was a difficult girl with a jealous, suspicious mind. She wasn't likely to change. Poor Andy, Dinah thought as she made her way home. He loved his wife, though. That was all that mattered. Judy would have no trouble at all in getting him back. Andrew would rush happily into his cage, eager to have his collar snapped back around his neck.

The rain had eased off considerably by the time Dinah got to her own flat. She walked up to the house and heard the thud-thud of Dilly's heaviest rock records. The actual tune couldn't be distinguished, but that deep bass note made the whole house shake from top to bottom.

She had a sudden bitter suspicion that when she let herself into the flat she would find Greg there, and her hand shook as she opened the front door.

Her glance flashed across the room and saw Dilly, in a black satin blouse and floppy white pants, dancing vigorously, her arms waving about like windmills.

She was alone. Dinah closed the door, weak with relief. "Hi," she said casually.

Dilly waved an arm, smiling with beatific contentment. "Saw you were back. The flat looks so tidy."

Dinah didn't comment on that. She sat down on the couch and watched as Dilly dipped and swayed. "Could we have that music down just a touch?" Dinah suggested mildly. "My eardrums are in danger of exploding."

"What?" yelled Dilly above the thudding beat.

"Can you turn it down before the neighbors storm the flat?"

"I can't hear you," Dilly said, switching the record player off.

"Who's surprised?" The silence was fantastic. Dinah drank it in with a deep sigh.

"What did you say?" Dilly asked, looking at her watch and giving an excited little murmur. "Sorry, I can't stop to talk. I've got to rush."

Dinah's whole body stiffened. "Got a date?" She was proud of herself for getting that out so calmly.

Dilly was at the door, flurried and with a hectic color. She glanced over her shoulder. "He's back, isn't he? He rang me the minute he arrived. And don't start giving me the gypsy's warning again, Dinah. I love him like crazy and nothing is going to stop me going over there."

She was gone with a slam of the door before Dinah could get out a syllable. Staring at the blank wall opposite her, Dinah thought of a number of epithets for Greg Randal. None of them seemed strong enough. She would have to invent some just for him.

Dilly's excitement, her happy anticipation, sank into Dinah like burning acid and left her with a sensation of sick misery all evening. The most painful part of it was her own jealousy. It was not pleasant to admit to herself that she was jealous. Jealous of Dilly! she thought, ready to kick herself. I really must be going out of my mind. Dilly, for heaven's sake!

Greg was never going to do more than amuse himself with Dilly, and Dinah didn't need a crystal ball to look into the future and know that one fine day Greg would drop Dilly like a discarded bus ticket. Unfortunately, knowing that didn't seem to make any difference. She was still jealous of *now*. What depths have I sunk to? she asked herself. That man has made me as emotionally irrational as Dilly herself.

She did not see Greg again for a week. To her relief, Sir Gee was back at his own desk, squinting at her through a cloud of cigar smoke. During her brief absence a lot had happened. Things always happened when Sir Gee was around. He briskly gave her an outline of events. He had bought up a smaller firm in one lightning move. Dinah knew he had had his eye on it, but she hadn't expected his takeover to happen yet. Sir Gee had been forced into action by the death of the controlling director.

"I'm sending Andrew to do some major reorganization," he told her. "A lot of things are wrong there. He'll have to shed some of their assets and whittle down the running expenses."

Dinah looked up, her blue eyes thoughtful. "Have you told him?"

Sir Gee chewed on his cigar. "Andrew? I'm seeing him this morning. Why?"

"I just wondered." The firm was based in York, several hundred miles away from London. "Andrew will be working up there from now on, then?"

Sir Gee made an impatient gesture, not interested in such a small detail. "Obviously."

A move like that might make all the difference to Andrew's chances of making his marriage work. Judy would know that with Dinah in London, at the other end of the country, Andrew would not be running to her all the time.

"Andrew will make a good job of it," she said, and Sir Gee nodded.

"He'd better, or I'll have Greg's head for it."

Dinah froze in her chair, her eyes fixed on his face. "Greg?" she repeated.

"He suggested Andrew. I was going to send Lewis Johnson. He's a tough hatchet man, just the type for this job. Still, we'll give Andrew his chance. He had better make good." Sir Gee only gave one chance. He expected his staff to work wonders. Sir Gee based his expectations of others on himself. He always worked flat out and so should everybody else, in his opinion.

Dinah went through to her own office half an hour later and sat down behind her desk. Greg had suggested sending Andrew off to York, had he? Wasn't that thoughtful of him?

Why had he done that? Or could she guess? Of course, it was possible Greg had merely been suggesting Andrew because he genuinely saw him as the right man for the job, but Dinah couldn't quite believe that. It didn't sound like the Greg Randal she knew at all. Greg had been interfering. Her instincts told her so. He was separating Andrew from Dinah with cold-blooded deliberation, because he disapproved of what he imagined their relationship to be and he had seen a chance of splitting them up.

What right did he think he had to do such a thing?

She was furious as she considered Greg's interference. The fact that he was way off course made no difference. He had meant to interfere—that was the point. Hypocrite, Dinah thought darkly. All his moral outrage over what he thought she had been up to, while all the time he was flirting cheerfully with poor little Dilly!

Andrew came down to see Sir Gee later that day. He talked to Dinah afterward, his face alight.

"It's fate," he told her. "Pure luck. I couldn't have planned it better myself."

"I'm glad you're pleased," said Dinah, watching his happy face. Well, at least someone was feeling great. Andrew looked as if he had been reborn. The lines of strain had gone from his face. His whole manner was calmer, easier.

"You see, I've seen Judy," he went on cheerfully. "She rang me at work and we had dinner. She's ready to try again, Dinah. Isn't that fantastic?"

"Fantastic," Dinah congratulated him, smiling. "I'm so happy for you, Andrew."

"And going to York will be just what we need," Andrew said, "It takes Judy right away from any danger of seeing this other guy again. She'll forget him." Andrew's face had a little flush. "She told me she had realized it was me, after all. She just got a little infatuated for a while. It didn't mean a thing, she said. She realized that almost right away. She missed me and she saw she had made a crazy mistake."

"Yes," Dinah said. What a liar Judy was, she thought.

"Nothing had happened between them," Andrew

told her. "Judy hadn't gone very far with him. It was all a brief infatuation. If we hadn't been quarreling all the time it would never have happened."

"I'm sure you're right," Dinah agreed with conscious irony.

"So we're going to turn over a new leaf," said Andrew. "I'll really make her happy this time if it kills me."

"I hope it won't do that."

He laughed. "Going to York is a stroke of luck, though. It will help us to get things straight between us."

"I'm sure it will."

"Hey, you won't need to worry about us," he told her. "And thanks for being ready to help. I really appreciate that. You won't need to bother now."

"No," Dinah said. So Judy hadn't told him that she had been to see her? Well, well, well. Judy was a very devious girl.

Andrew put both arms around her and gave her a kiss on the top of her hair. "Thanks for everything," he muttered before he bolted.

Chapter Eight

Greg showed up for a board meeting being held the following week. Dinah sat beside Sir Gee, a tape recorder at her elbow, recording the discussion between the directors, keeping her eyes on the slowly moving tape. Sir Gee was in one of his lively moods, good humor bubbling out of him, but none of the other men were taking any chances with him. You never knew when Sir Gee would give you a black glare. His temper was not always to be trusted.

His son was a chip off the old block, thought Dinah, listening to Greg tersely putting a point. You couldn't be sure of Greg Randal, either. He was unpredictable. At first sight she had written him down as a light-minded flirt, but he was a lot more than that. She watched him through her lowered lashes. He wasn't looking in her direction and she had an uninterrupted view of that hard profile.

He was as tough as his father. She should have known that from the strong, assertive structure of his face. That teasing little smile of his had given her the wrong impression of him.

Appearances could be very deceptive. Watching him now, he didn't look like the sort of man who would coolly flirt with a highly emotional teenager like Dilly. You could never tell about people.

Greg stopped speaking and turned in her direction. Dinah fixed her eyes on the tape. He wasn't going to catch *her* gazing at him like a lovesick schoolgirl.

Greg came down to Sir Gee's office after the meeting. Dinah took them some tea, her manner cool and polite, carefully skating her blue eyes past Greg without allowing them to linger as she handed him his cup.

She knew he watched her walking out of the room. Her spine prickled with the awareness of his narrowed stare.

Reception rang ten minutes later. Lady Randal was in the foyer and wanted to see her husband. "I'll come down," Dinah said. She made a point of escorting Lady Randal herself whenever Sir Gee's wife appeared at the office. It wasn't necessary, of course; Lady Randal knew the way to Sir Gee's office perfectly well. But it was a small courtesy which had grown up between them over the past year. Lady Randal was always careful to ring before arriving in the office and, recognizing the intended courtesy of that, Dinah was always careful to meet her and bring her along to Sir Gee personally.

One of the qualities which made Lady Randal so popular with everybody was her care in personal relations with the staff. She was always thoughtful, always considerate, and it paid dividends as far as the firm was concerned. Everyone was always happy to see her smiling face, especially Sir Gee.

Today Lady Randal was not alone. A girl stood beside her, her curly dark hair framing a pretty face which was yet oddly lifeless. After giving her a brief, assessing glance, Dinah greeted Lady Randal with a welcoming smile, and Lady Randal said to the dark girl, "Linda, this is Dinah, Sir Gee's secretary. He wouldn't know what to do without her now. She's his right-hand woman."

"I think that's you, Lady Randal," Dinah murmured, looking amused.

Lady Randal laughed. "We'll share the honors, shall we? We shan't tell Gee that a great man always needs an army of women behind him."

"Oh, he'd like the bit about a great man," Dinah said with a wry glance.

They both laughed, then Lady Randal told her, "Linda is my goddaughter. Her mother was at school with me."

Dinah's smile stiffened but she turned to shake hands with the other girl and felt a peculiar mixture of pain and bitter satisfaction as she met the brown eyes.

"How do you do?" Linda said limply. "It must be very interesting working for Sir George."

She's a bore, Dinah thought. Her voice was flat and dull, her eyes had no sparkle. I couldn't be more delighted, Dinah darkly decided. I hope she makes Greg very happy.

"I would like a job," Linda told her with all the enthusiasm of someone confronting a dull chore. "I ought to get one, don't you think, Aunt Maddie?"

"If you want one, dear, get one," Lady Randal said with a shrug. The android receptionist sat behind them, gazing into the jungle with her usual Mona Lisa smile. Lady Randal glanced at her and met Dinah's eyes. "Strange girl," she murmured. "She never seems to know who I am."

"She doesn't know who anybody is," Dinah reassured her. "They didn't get her programming right before she left the factory."

Lady Randal was still laughing under her breath as they walked into the lifts. "You must come down to Staunton one weekend, Dinah," she told her. "We ought to see more of you."

Dinah caught her eye and thought, The last thing I want to do is see any more of the Randal family. She did not say that, of course, but her blue eyes could be very articulate. Lady Randal gave her a shrewd smile.

"If you can stand Gee in your spare time," she added.

Dinah smiled discreetly. "How kind of you," she murmured in a noncommittal way.

She opened the door of Sir Gee's office to announce his wife, and Sir Gee bounded from behind his desk, all smiles. "Hallo, Maddie, what're you doing in town?" He kissed her cheek, looking as delighted to see her as though they hadn't met for weeks. "Nice dress," he flattered her. "Like that color. New, is it?"

"No, Gee. I've had it for months. I had it on at breakfast and you told me you liked it then."

"Well, I do," he said with a trace of sulkiness, and his wife viewed him with fond amusement.

Greg had risen, too, and was smiling at Linda. Dinah forced herself to watch. It would be good for her soul, she told herself. When she was a little girl her grand-mother had always said that. Eat your nice spinach, it will be good for your soul. At the age of six Dinah had got the fixed impression that spinach had powerful spiritual qualities. When she discovered it was just a vegetable she stopped eating it.

"How are you, Lin?" Greg was asking in a warm voice, that voice which sounded like melting honey and which was so different from the curt, terse way he always spoke to Dinah.

"Fine," Linda said. "Fine. How are you, Gregory?"

Gregory, Dinah thought. Well, that was his name, of course, but she had never heard anyone else use it. It sounded odd.

"I'm fine," he said.

"Oh, good." Linda sat down, arranging her pale green skirt with care. She looked up and gave Greg another demure little smile. "Super weather, isn't it?"

"Super," Greg said with zest.

"We had a lovely drive here," Linda expanded.

"Good," Greg said.

Sparkling conversation, thought Dinah. How they'll chatter over the toast and marmalade.

Turning to Greg's parents, she asked, "Can I get you some tea, Lady Randal?"

"Oh, please, I'm dying for some," Lady Randal agreed, and Dinah went out quietly, closing the door behind her and standing in her own office for a moment before she moved again. So that was the girl Greg Randal was going to marry one day? Wasn't he lucky? From the way she was dressed and her remark about feeling she ought to get a job, Dinah could imagine she came from a wealthy family. She would be a highly

145

eligible catch for Greg, no doubt, a very suitable girl
with just the right moneyed background. She was also a
very pretty girl, so long as you didn't expect witty
conversation. If she kept her mouth shut and just
smiled she would be an ornamental background for
Greg at parties. Dinah hoped Greg would be bored to
death. Serve him right, she thought grimly. She's just
what he deserves.

Over the next few days she forgot all about Lady
Randal's invitation to stay at Staunton, but a week or
so later Sir Gee looked up from a pile of paperwork as
Dinah was going home one day and said absently, "Oh,
I forgot. Maddie sent you a message."

"Yes?" Dinah asked, waiting while he ransacked his
memory for what his wife had said.

"Something she said at breakfast," he muttered,
scratching his ear. "Don't forget, she said."

Sir Gee had the worst memory for nonbusiness
details Dinah had ever met. She often thought he
forgot things deliberately. His rapid, shrewd mind
already had too much to carry. Sir Gee wasn't wasting
energy remembering small things as well.

"Weekend," he came up with triumphantly, looking
pleased with himself. "That was it. Come for the
weekend."

Dinah sought helplessly for some polite excuse.
"That's very nice of you," she began, and Sir Gee
beamed at her, satisfied with that grateful response.

"Good, good. I'll take you down with me on Friday
evening, then."

"But—" Dinah began again, and he waved a pater-
nal hand toward her.

"Nonsense, nonsense, happy to have you. Should have thought of the idea before. Maddie's right. Must see more of you, show you around Staunton." Having disposed of her, he buried himself in his paperwork again.

Dinah stood there unhappily for a few seconds, then realized that Sir Gee had forgotten her existence. She withdrew, biting her lower lip.

She did not want to go down to Greg's home for the weekend. The idea appalled her. What could she do? She must think of a good excuse for getting out of it, but what? And if she did come up with something, knowing Lady Randal's tenacity and warm hospitality, she would sooner or later be forced to go down there anyway. Lady Randal would not forget, even if Sir Gee would. He would forget the whole idea in two seconds flat she was sure. But not his wife. Lady Randal had a memory like an elephant.

She would have to go, she realized, and keep her fingers crossed that Greg would be spending the weekend elsewhere. Maybe he'd be spending the weekend with Linda. He spent some weekends down at his family home; but he also had a flat in town, which was his usual home, and on weekends he often went off to stay with friends in the country. He liked to get out of town, Sir Gee had told her once. "Greg has a busy social life," he had added, quite unnecessarily. Dinah had known that.

When she told Jennifer about the invitation, Jennifer looked envious. "Lucky beast. Staunton's fabulous, isn't it?"

"It's very attractive," Dinah agreed.

"You've been there before, though?"

"I've driven down with Sir Gee once or twice, but only for a short visit and always on business. He often takes visiting grandees there; we had some Americans over some months back who spent an evening there. I had dinner with them." Dinah laughed, remembering it. "Lady Randal needed a spare female for the dinner table—someone dropped out at the last moment—so they ordered me down to make up the numbers."

Jennifer sighed. "If the same thing happens this weekend, remember me. I'll make up numbers any time they like."

Dilly came in on the conversation toward the end of it and said, "What are you talking about?" She had just got in rather late and was wearing one of her gaudier outfits. She looked as if she had been appearing in a circus. Every time Dinah saw Dilly these days she could not imagine her with Greg. She tried, but it seemed so unbelievable. They just didn't go together at all. Why was Greg seeing her?

Jennifer opened her mouth to say, "Dinah's going to Staunton for the weekend," then caught Dinah's warning glance and stopped dead like a fish out of water and said nothing.

Dilly gazed expectantly at her. Dinah asked casually in the little silence, "Where have you been this evening? Had fun?"

"A disco," Dilly said, distracted. "It was great, but the strobe lights gave me a rotten headache. Is there any aspirin?"

"In the bathroom," Dinah reminded. She kept the bathroom cupboard stocked with basic medicines whenever she remembered. As she knew, such mundane precautions never occurred to Dilly, who was still at the stage of expecting someone else to provide her with what she might need in an emergency.

Dilly sauntered off and Dinah hissed, "Don't tell her," under cover of the running water in the bathroom. Dilly yelled, "Having a bath," and disappeared.

"You have to hand it to her—she's always clean," Jennifer said.

Andrew came into the office that Friday morning to say goodbye. Dinah was sad as she talked to him. Andrew was part of her life and now he was going away. When she left home to come up to London to work she had relied on Andrew's company to help her settle into city life. She felt as though she were losing part of herself, and although she knew it was a good move for him she had to force herself to look happy about it.

She wanted to say, "I'll miss you," but she decided it was wisest not to do that.

"You must come and stay with us," he invited.

A good thing Judy didn't hear that, decided Dinah. She smiled. "Love to." She wouldn't, of course. Judy would see to that, and Dinah had no intention of going, anyway. She had learned her lesson. Stay out of people's personal lives. From now on Andrew was on his own. He was a big boy now; he must manage his own life, which included his problems with his wife, Judy.

Andrew hugged her warmly as he was going. "I'll miss you, Dinah," he said as he kissed her ear, though he had meant it for her cheek. Dinah had turned her head hurriedly to avoid his kiss and found herself staring at Greg Randal as she looked across the room.

He was leaning in the door leading to his father's office, one hand flat against the doorframe, his long, lean body disposed with taut elegance as he stared at them.

Andrew turned, saw Greg and said cheerfully, "Just off, Greg—wish me luck."

"Good luck," Greg said with a wooden expression.

Andrew offered his hand, smiling, and Greg slowly extended his own. "Well," Andrew said, hovering on one foot and vaguely aware that the atmosphere had cooled by several degrees. "Well, I must rush, I suppose. 'Bye."

"Goodbye," Greg told him briskly.

Andrew looked at Dinah. "Goodbye, Andy," she said huskily, and Andrew nodded as he left, his face faintly melancholy. Andrew knew things were going to change. His old bolthole was no longer available to him. He was strictly on his own now and he felt a little lost, no doubt.

"Need a handkerchief?" Greg asked sarcastically from the door. Dinah threw him an icy smile.

"No, thank you. I don't."

"I didn't hear you telling him you'd miss him," he observed, watching her through half-lowered lids.

"Maybe you didn't start eavesdropping soon enough."

"I was not eavesdropping—I called in to find my father."

"He's at a meeting in the city with his bankers." Sir Gee loved meetings with his bankers. He had a peculiar enjoyment in squeezing money out of them. They always got it back, but they were always reluctant to hand it over, and Sir Gee enjoyed browbeating and coaxing them until they coughed up hard cash.

Greg muttered something under his breath. She didn't catch it and looked at him inquiringly. "What did you say?"

"I'd forgotten," he admitted. She thought he would go then, but instead he wandered over to stare out the window at the towering office blocks which edged the London skyline.

"I hear that Duncan has gone back to his wife," he murmured without turning around.

Dinah sat down at her desk and began to flip through a pile of papers. She saw no reason why she should answer that. Why didn't he go? She did not want him cluttering up her office all morning. She had work to do.

Greg waited, then said brusquely, "You'll get over it, you know."

Dinah did not want his patronizing kindness. She was about to say something stinging when the phone started to ring. Picking it up, she spoke in her usual cool, polite voice, and while she was talking Greg walked past her out of the room.

How did he know that Andrew and Judy were back together again? Where did he get his information from? It was incredible the way news got around in a firm as big as this—people you had never even met knew everything about you. Didn't any of them have anything better to do than gossip about the other members of the staff? Dinah tried to avoid eating in the canteen downstairs because, as Sir Gee's secretary, she was always under fire from other girls dying to know the secrets of the top floor. Dinah refused to let them prize any secrets out of her, of course, but she found it a bore to have to sit there and be interrogated over a chef's salad.

She had brought a small weekend case with her. Sir Gee carried it down in the lift, brushing aside her murmured denial. "I'll take it, I'll take it," he said. Sir Gee never minded repeating anything. It was his usual habit of speech. What was worth saying once was, in his opinion, even better said twice.

The chauffeur helped her into the back of the sleek limousine. Sir Gee climbed in and sank with a groan into the seat beside her.

"Hate weekends," he confided.

"Oh, dear," Dinah said, hoping he wasn't hating this one because she was going to be present.

"Boring," he said. "Small talk, visiting people. Maddie will organize things. Loves to be busy, my wife. People all over the place at weekends. Still, that's what she wants."

And what Lady Randal wanted was what Sir Gee made sure she got, Dinah finished for him, smiling as she looked out the window.

"Like walking?" he asked, and she glanced back to nod. Sir Gee looked pleased. "Walks," he suggested. "You and me—we'll go for walks, get away from all the bores. They stick around the house all day. We'll get out, take the dogs. Good exercise."

"That sounds nice," Dinah agreed, thinking that it would also mean she would get away from Greg if he happened to be one of the party.

"Right," said Sir Gee, smiling broadly. "It's a bargain. It will give us a chance to talk about the York operation. Andrew gave you his plans, did he?"

"He was only working on paper, remember," Dinah pointed out, not at all surprised to hear that Sir Gee meant to put her to work during the weekend. "When he's on the spot he may be much better informed."

"May be? He'd better be," Sir Gee muttered. "On paper it looks a mess."

When they got down to Staunton they found the long drive already crowded with cars. Sir Gee eyed them morosely. "Hordes of people again," he grunted.

The house was a tranquil Queen Anne building: red brick; flat, well-proportioned windows; a high, Dutch-style gable set under red tiles. Dinah could see a beautiful, huge cedar tree layering the summer sky beyond the house, sculptured black shadow from it thrown across the well-kept lawns. Bees droned heavily among closely set flower beds. The scent of summer and the warm silence seemed to fill the afternoon.

"I was born here, you know," Sir Gee said at her side. "My father bought it way back around the turn of the century. Made his money in soap. He wanted to move up in the world so he bought Staunton. I was born in the room up there." He pointed with one stubby finger. Dinah looked and saw the latticed windows and, behind them, crisp chintz curtains patterned with pink and green.

"It's beautiful," Dinah said gently.

Sir Gee sighed. "When it isn't full of people. Still, that's what Maddie likes. Likes people, my wife. Not that I don't, mind you, but moderation in all things, that's my motto."

Incredulous, Dinah looked at him. Did he really

believe he was moderate? How could he? He was the least moderate man she had ever known.

Sir Gee was already on the move. He could move like greased lightning when he chose. Dinah followed with a sense of doom. She wasn't at all looking forward to spending this weekend with the Randal family. She was going to have to face out this weekend, so she might as well accept the fact.

Sir Gee charged through the front door, yelling for his wife. Lady Randal appeared at the door of the drawing room, calm and smiling and placid.

"There you are," Sir Gee said, midyelp. "Wondered where you'd got to."

"Yes, here I am, Gee," she said, kissing his cheek.

Turning to Dinah, she smiled at her welcomingly. "I'm glad you could come, Dinah. It will be lovely to have you here. I'm glad that we'll have this time to spend together. We must find time for a chat. Would you like to see your room? Or would you like to relax and have a cup of tea first?"

"Tea," Sir Gee said, rolling forward. "Who's in there?" he asked, stopping before he got to the drawing-room door and lowering his voice to a conspiratorial mutter.

"Go in and see," Lady Randal ordered, shooing him off like a small boy.

Resigned, Sir Gee entered and Dinah and his wife came in his noisy wake as he gruffly said hello to his guests. Lady Randal introduced Dinah with a wave of her hand.

"You'll soon get to know everyone," she promised.

Dinah smiled around the crowded room. She was beginning to see what Sir Gee meant. Were they all staying here? Faces she did not recognize, a few she did, swam in front of her eyes.

The one which briefly fixed her gaze was that of Linda, who gave her a dull little smile of recognition. Greg was not present, Dinah was relieved to see. However, she did wonder where he was and if he were coming. She took the chair Lady Randal indicated and accepted her cup of tea and a wafer-thin sandwich.

"So you're Sir George's secretary," said the woman next to her. "How interesting it must be for you. Isn't he a wonderful man?"

"Wonderful," Dinah said.

"We live next door, the house with the green gables. Have you been to Staunton before?"

Dinah answered absently, her mind set on the conversation she could half hear between Lady Randal and Linda. The room was so crowded and everyone was talking, yet Dinah had picked up Greg's name across the room and was trying to catch what was being said about him.

"Quite unlike him," his mother said. "He's altered since he was over there. Two years is a long time, I suppose."

"I was in New York last year," Linda announced in her flat voice, "For two weeks."

"I remember," Lady Randal agreed.

"Greg took me to dinner. We had lobster."

"Oh," Lady Randal said. "How nice."

"It made me sick. Seafood does. I was ill all night."

"Oh, dear," said Lady Randal, staring at her. "You shouldn't have eaten it if you knew it made you ill."

"Greg said it was the specialty of the house. He said I ought to try it."

"Why didn't you tell him seafood made you sick?"

Linda looked blank. "He said I ought to try it."

"But didn't you explain?"

"No," Linda said. "I didn't like to say anything."

"Silly girl," said Lady Randal, shaking her head, a wry expression in her eyes. "You mustn't be scared of Greg. He takes after his father—he's very easy to manage once you know the way."

Linda did not look as though the idea that Greg took after Sir Gee was in any way reassuring. Her brown eyes moved to consider Sir Gee. He was eating cucumber sandwiches very fast, and in between each bite he was describing to a horrified lady next to him how his Alsatian behaved whenever it met another dog.

"Goes for the throat," he said approvingly. "Can't get her to open her jaws once she's got her teeth into anything."

"Goodness," his neighbor said, swallowing.

Dinah suppressed a smile and suddenly caught Lady Randal's eye across the room. Lady Randal was looking amused, too. For a second or two they smiled at each other; then Lady Randal's head lifted and she looked at the door behind Dinah with a warm smile.

"There you are, darling."

Everyone but Dinah turned to smile at the newcomer. Dinah already knew, without having to turn to look, that it was Greg who had entered the room. Lady Randal gestured for him to come into the room. "Have some tea," she invited. "Come and sit with Linda."

Dinah studied her teacup with fixed intensity. She had been hoping Greg wasn't coming at all. She should have known. Fate was in no mood to be kind to her just now.

Chapter Nine

Dinah came into the drawing room before dinner that evening, hoping to find the other guests already downstairs, but to her dismay found Greg alone in the room, standing in front of the fireplace with a glass of whiskey in his hand. She stopped dead, her long skirt rustling, half inclined to back out, but it was too late. His black head lifted and he shot her a grim stare.

"Oh, hello," she faltered.

His gray eyes traveled over her, moving from her smooth blond hair down over the black dress, leaving her with the feeling she had just been stripped visually. Her color rose in an angry flood.

"Drink?" he asked curtly. "Sherry?"

"Please," Dinah stammered. "Sweet sherry." Her anger could not diminish the fierce racing of her pulse. The physical effect he had on her was nothing short of disastrous. She couldn't believe the way his presence made her feel. He must know what he did to her with one of those narrow-eyed stares, and she didn't enjoy feeling a fool. She was behaving like a romantic school-girl. She did not like what was happening to her.

He walked over to pour her sherry, and Dinah stared at the lean, powerful figure in the dark suit, wishing she could stop looking at him and feeling like this, her whole body tensely aware of him, of every part of him, of every move he made.

He swung around to hand her the glass. Their fingers brushed and Dinah flinched, the touch of his skin searing on her own. Greg gave a harsh intake of breath. "For heaven's sake!"

Her eyes flickered, her lashes hiding her startled expression. She was still trembling from that brief touch, so she hurriedly sat down with her sherry in her hand.

"Let's have it out in the open," Greg bit out, standing over her as though he would love to shake her physically.

She froze in horror. "What?" Did he know how she felt? Was that what he meant? Could he sense her feelings? The idea that Greg might realize that she was crazy about him left her feeling sick.

"You're brooding over the fact that it was my idea to send Duncan to York, aren't you?" He moved with the restless, prowling lope of a caged animal, to and fro between her chair and the fireplace, his long body as taut as a bowstring. "I realize you blamed me once my father told me he had let it slip that it was my idea to send Duncan away."

Dinah sipped her sherry, but her hand was trembling

so much the amber liquid did not touch her lips. Her mouth felt numb as it slid against the glass.

"If he gave a damn for you, he would have taken *you* to York, not his wife," Greg said fiercely. "You've got to face it, Dinah. He chose her when it came down to it. That was wise of him, for all of your sakes." She didn't answer and he watched her, eyes glittering. "You make me angry, you know that? Why don't you admit it?"

Dinah forced herself to look at him, her brows lifting.

"Admit what? What are you talking about?"

"You were mad because I persuaded my father to send Andrew to York, weren't you?"

"Oh, that," Dinah muttered.

"Yes, that. You were furious, weren't you?"

"You had no right to interfere, but . . ."

"I knew you were resentful," Greg broke out before she could finish that sentence. "I've been getting icy looks from you ever since."

"I wasn't aware—" she began coolly, and he laughed with vicious dryness.

"You knew what you were doing. You always do. As Dilly says, you are one very cool lady."

Dinah's backbone stiffened and she carefully put her sherry down untouched on a nearby coffee table. "Talking about Dilly, if I were her father I think I'd be inquiring about your intentions any day now." She kept her tone well iced, and Greg reacted to it with a snarl of fury.

"You what? Who do you think you're talking to?"

Dinah stood up. This was one row she was not conducting sitting down. "I'm far too fond of Dilly to stand by and watch her getting her heart broken by a selfish beast like you."

"Dilly's heart is in no danger from me," Greg snapped.

"I wish I could believe that. Of course, I find it difficult to credit that any girl with a modicum of intelligence would so much as look twice at you, but Dilly isn't exactly an adult yet. She's young enough to make a fool of herself over you."

"You flatter me," Greg said through his clenched teeth.

"Not in a million years," Dinah retorted. "I'm not in the habit of flattering men like you."

"Men like me," he repeated. "All right, I'll stick my neck out. Why not? You can only chop it off once. Men like what, Miss Trevor?"

"Don't tempt me." She was almost inarticulate from the sheer pressure of the epithets building up inside her brain.

"Now there's a thought." He smiled with deliberate, cold menace, letting his gaze wander over her in a sensual appraisal which caught her on the raw.

"Don't kid yourself!" she almost yelled at him, her voice hoarse with a mixture of fury and pain.

"Frustrated women get very difficult," he murmured, watching her.

"Frustrated . . ." Dinah could have hit him, her gasp of rage stifled before she had done more than repeat the word. "I am not frustrated."

"As I said, you have to face it—Duncan has gone back to his wife. He preferred her." Greg smiled tightly at her. "Sorry if that hurts." He hardly sounded sorry. He sounded as though nothing could delight him more.

He was enjoying himself, tormenting her, as he imagined, with Andrew's departure. Dinah looked at him with blazing eyes and thought, I hate you, Greg Randal, I really hate you.

"Heaven knows what you saw in him, anyway," he flung at her as he met her angry stare. "He was as thick as two short planks."

"Andrew was nothing of the kind!"

"You leap to his defense very rapidly," he said with a chilling smile. "Does he call out the maternal impulse in you? Is that it? You like weak men, do you?"

"Andrew's not weak." Well, she mentally adjusted, not exactly weak. It was only in his relationships with the women in his life that Andrew was so pliable, so unable to cope.

"No? I'd say that was just what he was," Greg muttered. "Anyone with an ounce of spirit could knock him down and walk all over him."

"If you're talking about yourself, I imagine Andrew did find you pretty nasty," Dinah agreed with malice. "He isn't the type to know how to deal with a bully."

"Thank you." His voice was restrained but his eyes were like hot metal. "You're too kind. I can't recall anyone ever telling me to my face that I was a bully, but new experiences are always good for one. Don't you think?"

"Don't be so pompous!"

"Oh, I'm pompous, too, am I? Carry on," he invited. "As this is obviously home truths day, why not finish your little list? What else is wrong with me?"

"There aren't enough hours in the day for me to tell you."

Dinah hadn't realized how sharply and loudly she

was speaking until a movement behind her made her turn her head around. Lady Randal stood stiffly at the door, staring at them both with a startled, incredulous expression. In the deadly silence which followed Dinah heard the reverberations of their argument inside her own head. The whole house must have heard them quarreling. Only now did she realize how loudly they had been shouting at each other, and her flushed face burned with embarrassment.

"Oh, hell," Greg said tersely, slamming out the door and passing his mother without a glance.

"Dinah, dear, what has been going on?" Lady Randal came forward slowly, eyes wide and curious.

"I'm sorry," Dinah muttered, moving toward the door herself with the intention of bolting back upstairs. She ran into Sir Gee, who steadied her by the arms, looking at her bolt-eyed.

"Hallo, what's up? What's up? Greg nearly knocked me down as he passed and he had a face like a thundercloud."

Lady Randal had recovered her calm smile. "Sherry, Gee?" she suggested. "Will you please pour me a glass, too?"

Sir Gee grunted. "First I want to know . . ."

"Sweet sherry, Gee," his wife pressed gently.

He met her eyes, blinking. "Oh, yes, yes, of course, Maddie." He went over and poured sherry while Dinah found herself being drawn by Lady Randal to the brocade-covered sofa.

"Tell me," Lady Randal said as she took her sherry from Sir Gee, "how was Paris looking when you were over there, Dinah?"

162

Some of the other guests arrived before Dinah had finished speaking. One of them took up something she had said about Paris, and the conversation became general, anecdotes of visits to France occupying them all for the next quarter of an hour. Even Linda contributed something when she arrived. "I got lost in Paris," she said with her usual flat absence of charm. Everyone waited, staring at her, but she appeared to have nothing to add.

"Did you, dear?" Lady Randal prompted.

Linda nodded. "I couldn't get a taxi so I walked and I got lost. I took hours to get from the Opera to the Left Bank. I think I went the wrong way."

"You must have done," one of the others agreed. "Simple to walk from the Opera—just keep straight on going."

"It can be very hard to get taxis in Paris," someone else murmured.

"I couldn't," Linda said, and again everybody looked at her and waited, but she just looked back, brown eyes vacant.

Dinah glanced at Lady Randal. Was she crazy to picture her son married to that girl?

Greg walked in just as they were all taking their places around the dinner table. To Dinah's relief he did not sit anywhere near her. She had Sir Gee on one side of her and a quiet man in a gray suit on the other. He said almost nothing. Sir Gee said a good deal, most of it muttered to her out of the corner of his mouth and a lot of it highly libelous about his other guests. He appeared to imagine none of them could hear him, but Dinah saw some of them getting very flushed as the meal wore on, their eyes bent on their plates. They did not try to protest, however. Meekly they suffered the slings and arrows of his insults. Sir Gee had a terrifying habit of speaking the truth which left them unable to say a syllable.

He carried Dinah off to a corner with him after dinner to talk about the firm they had taken over in York. Lady Randal gave her a sympathetic, grateful look during the long discussion. Dinah was keeping Sir Gee happy and out of harm's way. Everyone benefited. Sir Gee bored was a dangerous sight, enough to make strong men weep.

It was a relief when Dinah felt she could politely say good night and slip off to bed. Greg hadn't even looked at her all evening. And she was glad of having had no futher confrontation with him. His attention had been given to Linda, but Dinah had noticed with gleeful malice that Greg had had to work like mad to get much out of her. Conversing with Linda was like pushing a snowball up a hill.

Lady Randal met her in the hall the next morning after breakfast and said, "Do you feel like a walk, Dinah?"

Why do I get the feeling I'm here just to keep Sir Gee otherwise occupied until the other guests have safely left? Dinah thought, but she smiled and nodded. She could stand Sir Gee for hours, thank goodness. She had had to for the past year, after all.

"Good, so do I," Lady Randal said, astonishing her. "I'll take you across the spinney to see the view from Morden Wood Hill."

"Is Sir Gee coming?" asked Dinah, puzzled.

"He's talking about the stock market with Peter," his wife explained. "Come along, Dinah."

Dinah had a nasty feeling she was about to get the third degree. Lady Randal's curiosity had been awakened during Dinah's row with Greg and she was going to question Dinah closely during their walk.

There was no way out of it now, though. Dinah would have to grin and bear it.

The spinney was alive with birds, their flickering shadows half glimpsed among the close-set branches, their song coming from every side. "We get a lot of snakes here, too," Lady Randal told her. "Adders, I'm afraid, but contrary to popular belief they keep out of people's way as much as possible. You don't often find them on the paths."

Dinah shuddered. "I hope we don't run into any. I don't like snakes."

"People don't," agreed Lady Randal. "A primitive fear, the fear of snakes. We all have it, don't we? And it isn't very fair to snakes. Some sort of buried race memory, I suppose."

"I don't know about that—I just find them creepy," Dinah said. "It's the way they slither along. They frighten me." She paused. "Mice, too. I don't like the way they scamper around. My legs turn to jelly."

"Rats," Lady Randal said, and Dinah looked at her in surprise. Lady Randal laughed. "That's what I can't stand. Rats—and it's their long tails which make me shiver."

Smiling, Dinah nodded. "I know what you mean, not that I've ever seen many rats."

"We get a lot here in the country—they come from the barns." Lady Randal paused as Dinah negotiated a stile at the end of the spinney.

Dinah turned to walk on and Lady Randal said, joining her, "What's going on between you and Greg?"

It hit like a thunderbolt, even though she'd been expecting it. Dinah's face washed with hot color. "Oh," she mumbled, too disturbed to say any more.

"I've never seen him look so angry," his mother said in a strange tone.

"You haven't looked." Dinah bit that out before she had had time to consider her answer and then wished she hadn't.

"Obviously," Lady Randal said, watching her. "Is he in love with you, Dinah?"

Aware of the heat burning in her face, Dinah said huskily, "Good heavens, no," then asked even more unsteadily, "Why should you think that?" She had a lunatic flicker of hope for a second at the very idea, but then she remembered Greg's stony expression last night. That wasn't the look of love. That was the look of hostility.

"Why were you having that row, then? What was it all about?"

"Oh, nothing," Dinah muttered.

"Nothing? I can't believe Greg would yell at you over nothing, Dinah."

"You don't know him!" She could have bitten her tongue at the absurdity of saying that to his mother. Lady Randal merely looked amused, however, her eyes twinkling.

"I'm begining to wonder if I do—ever since he got

back from the States he's been so different. He went away a lively, charming companion and he's come back like a bear with a sore head."

"I thought he had always been like that!" Dinah walked on very fast, suddenly not caring very much if Lady Randal was offended by what she said. It no longer seemed to matter.

"No," his mother said, appearing at her side again. "Greg has only been in this mood since he got back from New York. I'd been wondering what was wrong with him. He isn't eating and his temper is always bad."

Dinah could have pointed out that Sir Gee was hardly an angel of sweetness and light, but Lady Randal knew that. Dinah didn't have to point out the obvious.

They had arrived at the top of a thickly grassed hill. It swept down to a valley hundreds of feet below. Black and white cows grazed under the interlaced branches of elms looking so content, and the colored jigsaw puzzle of the fields lay open to the sun as far as the eye could see. Barley and wheat fields held little scarlet glints of poppies, the golden sway of the stalks turning the view into a whispering sea as the wind rustled gently through them.

"You're right, this view is worth the climb," Dinah said, faintly out of breath as she paused.

"I thought you would like it." Lady Randal gazed down at the valley in proprietorial affection. "I often come up here. There's an air of peace about the landscape, isn't there? A certain tranquillity. You know, Dinah, those fields have been harvested for centuries. There's something reassuring about knowing that, don't you think? Human beings are very temporary creatures, but the land goes on forever."

A delicate tapering spire pierced the blue sky on the right side of the valley. Dinah asked, "How old is that church, do you know?"

"Twelfth century," Lady Randal told her. "The waterspouts have gargoyles carved on them—local legend has it that they were carved by a local stonemason and he used local faces. If that's true, there were some very ugly people around here in the twelfth century."

Dinah laughed. "An early cartoonist, perhaps."

"Very possibly," Lady Randal agreed. "I often look at the faces in that village and wonder whose ancestors had to see themselves staring down from the church walls every time they went past, and what they thought about it."

"I shouldn't think the stonemason was a very popular man," said Dinah.

"Talking about me?"

Dinah swung around at the sound of that voice, her heart flying up into her throat. Greg stood behind her, casually dressed in black jeans and a thin white polo-necked sweater, his hair blown into ruffled peaks after his climb. Had he followed them? she wondered. She hadn't heard anyone; but then, she had not been listening.

"A beautiful morning," Greg murmured, sliding his eyes down over the sunny landscape. "Just the morning for a quiet private chat. Mother, Dinah and I have a lot to talk about, so why don't you walk back home without us?"

"Yes, dear," his mother said cheerfully while Dinah stiffened in horror.

"We don't have anything to talk about," she said, but Greg calmly said, "Yes, we do."

"No, we don't," Dinah broke out, her voice unsteady.

"Yes, we do," Greg said again.

Lady Randal began to move away and Dinah shakily tried to follow, her legs weak beneath her. Greg grabbed her arm in the vise of his powerful fingers.

"Let go!"

Lady Randal didn't look around. She was walking briskly, her path toward the spinney. "Lady Randal," Dinah appealed to her. "Please wait for me."

Greg's fingers tightened and she winced, glaring at him. "Leave me alone. You're hurting me."

"Good. It may bring you to your senses."

"Will you let go of my arm?" Dinah spat out, wrenching at her imprisoned arm and completely unable to free herself.

Lady Randal had reached the stile and was deftly climbing over it. In a moment she would be out of sight and out of earshot. Dinah called after her, voice trembling with fury and pleading. "Please wait, Lady Randal."

"My mother is a sensible woman," Greg told her with unveiled satisfaction as he watched his mother disappear among the thickset trees. "She knows when a man means what he says."

"If she imagines I want to talk to you she's wrong," Dinah muttered, eyeing him with loathing. "I can't stand the sight of you for even five minutes. I've no intention of discussing anything with you."

"It's my intentions that count," Greg threw back, his mouth twisting in a crooked little smile.

Dinah watched him warily. "And what are they?"

"I told you—to talk." A mocking little gleam entered his eyes. "Unless you had other ideas?"

"I didn't," Dinah said, fire in her cheeks.

"I'm always open to suggestion," he teased.

"I'm sure you are." She met his smiling eyes with fury. "But I'm not."

"No," he said mournfully. "So I'd noticed."

"I'm glad you have noticed. I was beginning to wonder if I wasn't making myself clear enough." She used her iciest voice, her blue eyes chilling, and the smile vanished from Greg's face.

"Don't make me angry, Dinah, not this morning. I got up in a particularly sunny mood and I wouldn't advise you to make me lose my temper, like you seem to have a habit of doing."

"If it's going to make you lose your temper if I refuse to flirt with you, that's too bad," Dinah informed him. "I am not the flirtatious type."

"Now we're coming to a subject which has intrigued me for weeks," Greg said. "Just what type are you, Dinah?"

The question threw her for a moment. She stared at his hard, intent face, searching his eyes in an attempt to find out what lay behind the question.

He waited, and in the end she said flatly, "I suppose I'm not a type at all—I'm myself, a person, not a type, and I don't like being treated as though I were some sort of Identikit woman. Men who flirt with every woman they meet are insulting, whether they know it or not, because they aren't treating the woman as a human being, just a sex object. And I don't wish to be treated as such."

Greg's brows flicked together. "I don't see you as a sex object."

"You could have fooled me."

His frown deepened. "I take you very seriously, believe it or not."

Her dry stare made it clear she did not believe him. "Were you taking me seriously the day you flew back from New York and walked into your father's office?" She laughed angrily. "No, you weren't, Mr. Randal. You started flirting with me on sight, when all you knew about me was what you saw in the first two minutes."

He slowly ran his eye over her slender figure. "What's so strange about that? You're well worth looking at. . . ."

Her skin burned at the speculative survey. "Do you expect me to be flattered? I'm not."

"I wasn't flattering you. I was being truthful," he said with a glint in his eye.

Her blue eyes flashed. "That must be a first."

Greg drew a harsh, low breath. "You have a high opinion of me, don't you?"

"My opinions are my affair."

"Not when they concern me, they're not," he grated. "What have I ever done to you to get that sort of vicious comment?"

"Not to me," Dinah agreed. "To Dilly."

His eyes hardened. "Dilly again!"

"Yes, Dilly." Dinah met the angry rake of his eyes with her head lifted in defiance.

"Why do you keep bringing her up? What do you

171

think I am?" His voice was rough with temper and his face had a compressed rage in it as he watched her.

"Your father's my boss," Dinah said tartly. "I'd rather not tell you."

"Don't let that stop you," Greg invited harshly. "It hasn't in the past, at least, not that I can recall."

"Your memory is poor, then. I've been very careful to keep my opinion of you to myself."

"You got it over, even so," Greg said. "I was never under any illusions about what you thought of me."

"Well, that's a relief," Dinah said sarcastically, and Greg moved with the speed of light, his hands clamping down on her arms, yanking her toward him so fast she did not have time to think, let alone protest.

Stupefied, she looked at him with eyes so wide they stretched her smooth skin. Greg stared into them, hypnotized, the anger fading from his face for a moment.

"You're going to listen to me, like it or not," he said huskily. "So just stand there, Dinah, and stop needling me."

"I don't want to listen to you," Dinah muttered in a shaken voice, furious with herself because she could not be unaware of his physical magnetism when he held her so close, their bodies almost touching in that intimate contact.

"Damn you, you're going to," Greg flared, his fingers tightening as he half shook her to enforce the fierce determination of his words. "You're going to listen if I have to nail it through your obstinate head!" He glared down at her. "Have you got that, Dinah? Do you understand what I'm saying?"

She looked away, her throat closed in breathless tension. "Yes," she said weakly, hating herself for that weakness. A crow flapped on ragged wings across the blue sky, and Dinah followed the effortless flight without knowing what she was looking at, her nerves leaping with fierce awareness.

Chapter Ten

Greg gave a long sigh, his fingers relaxing their grip slightly. "Thank you," he said with dry emphasis. "To begin with what seems to be occupying your mind most—Dilly. Dilly and I had an arrangement."

Dinah took a painful breath. "What sort of arrangement?"

"Not what you seem to imagine," he said angrily. "Dilly just wanted to talk to someone."

"She wanted to do what?" Dinah couldn't stop the angry laughter which broke out of her. Greg's eyes watched her with a metallic glitter.

"I'm not being funny."

"No," she agreed, "you're not."

"Listen, you cynical idiot, Dilly needed to talk to someone who wouldn't tell her not to be silly or shut her up every time she brought up a certain name!"

Dinah looked sharply at him. "What?"

"Hamish," Greg said.

"Hamish," repeated Dinah stupidly, her lips parted in disbelief. "She talked to you about Hamish?"

"All the time," he said. "I gather you and Jennifer lectured her every time she mentioned him to either of you."

"He's no good for her," Dinah insisted tartly.

"She loves him."

"He uses her as a convenient doormat, unpaid labor. She does all his domestic work for him, ironing his clothes, cleaning, and waits on him hand and foot, but when Hamish gets bored he goes off with other girls."

"She loves him," Greg repeated.

"He's bad-tempered, too," Dinah came out, glaring at him.

"I know." Greg grinned, fingering his jaw. "I found out the hard way."

Dinah's eyes widened.

"Hamish is back in London," Greg informed her. "Dilly and I were having a drink when Hamish walked in and knocked me right across the room."

"Hamish knocked you across a room?" She measured his wide shoulders, his deep chest, the formidable length of his body. "I don't believe Hamish is capable of such a thing."

Greg grimaced. "I didn't for a minute, myself. He's about five foot three and built like a matchstick. The whole bar went quiet. I got to my feet feeling as if I'd been hit by a runaway truck. Dilly was hanging on to Hamish and begging him not to do it again, and when I stood up Hamish told me in a thick Glasgow accent that if he saw me with her again he'd break me into little pieces and eat what was left."

Dinah took a hurried breath. "What did you do?"

"Are you kidding? I left."

She was too staggered to say anything. The last thing she had ever imagined from Greg was cowardice.

He gave her a wry grin. "You think I should have taken him on? What would have been the point? I already looked pretty silly, but if I'd got into a real fight with him Dilly might have suffered. I didn't want that. I left her with him because that was what Dilly wanted. Her face was shining like the rising sun. She was in heaven. Hamish had been jealous, don't you see? Dilly loved every minute of it."

"He's dangerous," Dinah erupted. "A temper like that—how could you leave Dilly with him?"

Greg surveyed her. "To put it in Dilly's own language—he's her man. Do you know what that means, Dinah, or do you need some sort of blueprint before you understand?"

She blushed, her eyes evading the mockery of his stare. "Dilly's half a child," she protested.

"Dilly is all woman," he drawled. "Where Hamish is concerned. She knows what she wants. It bothered her that you and Jennifer—but particularly you, because she admires you—were always nagging her to drop Hamish. Always telling her he was no good. She couldn't reason with you because Dilly isn't very lucid, but her feelings are sound. She knew how she felt. She just didn't know how to get it across to you and Jennifer. She didn't know what to say to make either of you believe what she felt."

Dinah hesitated. "You did flirt with her, though, didn't you?"

He shook his head. "If she told you I did, she was just throwing up a smoke screen."

That was possible, of course. Dilly wasn't above being devious, as Dinah knew.

"Maybe she wanted to give herself a little status," Greg said with a grin. "I think she rather liked going around to London's nightspots with me."

Giving him a tart look, Dinah said, "Modesty isn't your strong point, is it?"

He shrugged. "I've got a glamorous background, and, let's face it, money is always glamorous to a girl like Dilly. Why not? She liked going around in my sports car and drinking champagne and having a first-class time."

"You did pull out all the stops," muttered Dinah. "Champagne and caviar, no doubt."

He didn't deny it, his face rueful. "Why not? She has an amazing capacity for enjoying herself. I liked watching her react to it all. She let herself go and had a wonderful time. She hasn't any inhibitions, has she? She flings herself into whatever comes her way. It was fun for both of us. I liked watching her have such a good time, and she liked having me take her around."

"I'm sure she did." She couldn't help the tart ring of her voice, and Greg shot her a sideways smile.

"Careful; you might sound the tiniest bit jealous to anyone less modest than myself," he said with a smile in his eyes.

Her cheeks burned. "Don't kid yourself." Hurriedly, she asked, "When did Hamish get back from Scotland?"

"While we were in Paris."

So it had been Hamish Dilly had been talking about when she said, "He's back." Dinah vividly remembered that defiant look and she had thought Dilly had been talking about Greg.

"Dilly really does need to see a psychiatrist. Hamish will only make her miserable again."

"Don't interfere," advised Greg. "She worships the ground he stamps on—and, however badly he treats her, I think he cares quite a bit for her, too. Hamish is older than she is, remember. He's in his twenties and Dilly is so much younger. I don't think Hamish is ready to settle down yet, but when he *is* ready it's going to be Dilly he ends up with, I'm certain. I've seen them together now. He sees her as his property, and when a man thinks about a woman like that, he's had it."

"I don't understand it," Dinah murmured absently, feeling the morning sunshine on the back of her neck and shifting away from the direct heat of the sun.

"Don't you, Dinah?" Greg's voice was low and husky.

She stiffened, looking at him in sudden uneasiness. "We'd better get back, hadn't we? It must be getting quite late."

"Not yet," Greg said, his face tightening. "First, having cleared up your worry over Dilly, can we clear up the other issue?"

She regarded him warily. "What other issue?"

"Andrew Duncan."

Her blue eyes iced over. "I've told you before . . ."

"You've told me, but the evidence of my own eyes contradicts what you've said."

"You're mistaken. I've told you—Andrew and I are

friends. I've known him most of my life. There's nothing between us."

"I'd like to believe you," Greg said in a voice which indicated that he didn't believe one single word of it.

"I don't care whether you do or not," Dinah flung at him. "Look, his mother and mine have been friends for over thirty years. Since Andy and I were tiny we've been buddies. Okay? Just like brother and sister, like I've told you before. That's all there is to it. Every time he fell for some girl he would ask my advice and I'd give him tips on how to handle his romantic problems. Andy hasn't got a clue about women."

"Him and me both," Greg said tersely.

"Oh, you do, all right," Dinah retorted with intense irritation. "I've never noticed you running into any problems."

"Then you haven't been looking," he told her.

"Andy is a good executive, though. He can stand up to Sir Gee because he does what he's told and never flaps. He doesn't need to flap in the office. Any problem that comes up is easily handled—he finds out what Sir Gee wants him to do and he does it. It's as simple as that."

Greg gazed at her, dumbfounded. "And you call that a good executive? The man's nothing but a ninny."

Dinah smiled wryly. "Andrew will never set the world on fire," she agreed. "But he does his job."

"I hope he manages to handle the York assignment on his own," Greg observed. "He won't have my father around to tell him what to do up there."

"Someone will," Dinah said simply. "Someone always tells a man like Andy."

179

Greg considered her, his face intent. "That certainly doesn't sound like the voice of a woman who's madly in love."

She met his eyes. "Believe me, I'm not and never have been in love with Andy."

"Then what was going wrong with his marriage?"

She sighed. "Well . . ."

Greg frowned. "Well, what? Why the guilty expression?" His eyes had hardened again.

"To be frank, his wife got the same impression you got," she murmured reluctantly.

"Ah," Greg said through his teeth, scowling.

"No," Dinah denied, shaking her head. "Once I realized what she suspected I went around to see her, and she believed me in the end. That's why she went back to him."

Greg watched her face like a cat at a mousehole. "And that honestly isn't bothering you? That his marriage is on again?"

"I'm delighted," Dinah insisted.

"Then why have you been so evil-tempered lately?" Greg inquired with a wicked glint in his eye.

Dinah could not control the flush which swept over her face. Her blue eyes shifted away from him, but her pulses were beating at her throat and wrists and she was having great difficulty in breathing with any comfort. "Have I been? Sorry."

"You don't deny it, I notice," Greg told her, his eyes suddenly brilliant in the sunlight, his hard features softening in a smile which changed his whole face.

Dinah was sarcastic. "I've been trained never to argue with my boss." She paused. "Or even his son," she added.

Greg laughed, giving her an amused look. "But if you were never involved with Andrew Duncan you've had someone else on your mind," he went on coolly, watching the way her eyes widened and fell, the way her color deepened again. "Or you've been giving a very good imitation of a woman in love," he drawled.

"Nonsense," Dinah said, hoping her voice wasn't shaking as much as she was afraid it was.

"Even my father noticed," Greg said, and Dinah looked at him in amazement.

"Sir Gee?"

"Of course, he put it down to different causes. He just said he was afraid you were sickening for something lately. He hoped it wasn't catching." The gray eyes were teasing her, and she reacted with angry panic, horrified at the idea that Greg had guessed how she felt.

"I've been very busy, that's all." Her voice had a curt ring to it, but Greg didn't seem to take much notice of it.

He put a hand to her sun-warmed cheek, his fingertips gently caressing the curve of it. "Stop snapping, Dinah."

"Don't!" She moved away, trembling.

"Why do you think I was so keen to send Duncan off to York? When my father started discussing who to send, it came to me like a bolt from the blue. I couldn't believe it. I jumped at the chance to get rid of Andrew Duncan. I hadn't anticipated that he and his wife would get back together again, of course, but I wanted badly to separate him from you."

Dinah tried to control the rapid pace of her pulses. "Then you wasted your energy, didn't you?"

"Maybe," he agreed. "If you were never together in the first place . . ."

"We weren't."

"I believe you," he said quickly. "Dinah . . ." His hand slid to her waist, and she pushed it away with a little gasp.

"No!" Her blue eyes met his. "Greg, if you're about to make me some sort of proposition, you can stop right there and forget it. I'm not interested. So please, just let me be."

"Dinah," he began again, and she glared at him intensely.

"I think we should be getting back to the house. I don't want your father sending out a rescue party for us."

"He won't." Greg dismissed the idea with a cavalier shrug. "He won't even notice we aren't there. Once my father is engaged in talking about money to someone whose brains he can pick he forgets everything else."

Dinah chose to be icy about that. "I am very fond of your father," she informed him coldly.

Greg grinned at her. "I had noticed that. I think it's mutual. We'll talk about my father later. I want to talk about us."

"There's no need to say any more," Dinah almost yelled at him.

"I don't have to, do I?" Greg was laughing under his breath. "You already know."

"I can guess," she admitted icily. "And the answer is no."

"I haven't asked the question yet." His other hand was sliding over her shoulder. She gave a shaken gasp as it descended lower.

"Get your hands off me! Don't you understand English?"

"I speak four languages," he said in mock earnestness. "*And* I can make myself very clear without any words at all."

"I'm getting your message, but my answer is the same—no, no, no!" His fingers were touching her in a way which made her whole body burn, and she wished she could be entirely indifferent to that warm, coaxing caress.

"I'm in love with you, Dinah," he whispered, and shock sent waves of heat pounding through her.

Their eyes met. Dinah couldn't say a word. Her lips were dry and trembling.

"From the minute I saw you," Greg said. "I fancied you the minute I walked into my father's office and saw a cool, offhand blonde giving me the frozen stare of someone determined not to be impressed." He grinned at her. "You were, weren't you? Determined not to give an inch. From the word go I was getting nothing but ice from you."

Her eyes confused, she couldn't deny it.

"When we were in Paris I was going around the bend," he said. "I'd hoped that if I got you on your own, without Duncan around to cloud the issue, I might be able to get through to you."

"You hoped you could seduce me, you mean," she retorted, anger in her face.

Greg looked at her impatiently. "Didn't you hear what I just said? I love you."

"I don't know what you mean by love," she began, and Greg caught her chin in one hand, silencing her, his eyes glittering.

"This is what I mean," he said, bringing his mouth down fiercely over hers. The ruthless, burning kiss caught her off guard. After a few seconds of resistance she surrendered to it, one arm around his neck, her fingers running up into his thick hair and curling in possessive excitement as she returned his affection.

When Greg stopped kissing her she was barely able to breathe, her heart knocking against her ribs, her ears singing with the rush of her blood.

"Dilly would be able to tell you," Greg said unevenly. "You're my woman, she would say. That's the only thing that matters, Dinah. That's what I mean by love—and for all your quick wits and your intelligence you have a lot to learn about that, I'm afraid."

Dinah gave a deep sigh, putting her head against his chest, the sound of his quick-beating heart under her ear.

"Dilly's uninhibited, as you said." She paused, sighing again. "I *am* inhibited, Greg. I couldn't just take up an affair with you. I'm not like that at all. I'd hate myself too much. I'd lose all my self-respect in a situation like that. Affairs seem to me to be far too painful and far too short-term."

"How about life?" Greg asked, his mouth moving against her hair.

Dinah wasn't sure what he meant. "What about it? If you mean that I'm not living unless I have an affair—"

"I mean would life be long-term enough?" Greg interrupted, laughing.

"What?" She lifted her head to look at him searchingly, her eyes a deep blue.

"Marry me," Greg said offhandedly, something in the way he said it reminding her strongly of his father.

"Marry you?"

"And don't repeat everyting I say like a parrot," Greg said brusquely. "Just answer yes or no."

"Marry you," Dinah said, her whole body weak. Then she groaned. "We couldn't. Your mother."

"What about my mother? Don't you like her?" Greg looked affronted.

"I love her," Dinah said. "But she wants you to marry Linda."

Greg's jaw dropped. "She *what?*"

"Wants you to marry Linda," Dinah said. Didn't he know?

"You've got to be joking! My mother wouldn't be so silly." Greg laughed, throwing back his dark head, his eyes full of incredulous amusement.

"She does," insisted Dinah.

"Who told you that?"

"Your father," Dinah said, frowning.

Greg gave another roar of amusement. "Dinah, I love you beyond belief, but here and now let me tell you that if you take any notice of anything my father says you need your head examined."

She regarded him warily. "It isn't true?"

"Not a word of it."

"But he said . . ."

"My father never knows what's going on in my mother's head—don't you realize that? For years he's bought her milk chocolates when she only eats dark ones. He just gets fixed ideas and sticks to them like glue. Mother understands him like the back of her hand, but Father doesn't have the slightest clue about her."

"Oh," Dinah said, too staggered to say more.

He cupped her head with one hand, looking into her blue eyes. "Linda bores me to tears. She bores my mother to tears. Have you got that?"

"I think so," she said, smiling.

"My mother likes you. Why do you think she lured you up here for me?"

"She did what?"

"Lured you up here," he said unashamedly. "We had a chat last night when everyone else was in bed and I told her how I felt. She promised to give me a chance to talk to you on your own where nobody could interrupt."

Dinah was almost shocked. "How very devious of her—she didn't give me the slightest idea."

"My mother is a very clever woman," Greg said with unhidden pride. "Everyone thinks it's my father who's clever. They don't know who pulls his strings."

Dinah's lips curved in a smile. "I had noticed a little string pulling from time to time."

"You can pull mine whenever you like," Greg offered with a mocking little grin. "After we're married, of course."

Dinah's breath caught. "You do take things for granted, don't you?"

His face lost the smile and his eyes were dark and intent. "I love you, Dinah. Just now I got the feeling it just might be mutual."

"Oh, did you?" She tried not to smile, but her quivering lips betrayed her and her blue eyes looked at him in a way which made his face blaze with excited passion.

"Dinah," he muttered, his arms going around her. "Oh, Dinah, I am crazy about you." His face touched her hair and he held her closer, breathing fast. "Tell me I'm not imagining things."

She slid her hands up his shoulders and curved her arms around his neck. Huskily, she told him. It wasn't easy to get the words out. Dinah hated admitting emotion. Her voice quivered as she said it. "I love you."

"Darling," Greg groaned, bending his head to search for her lips. The warm summer morning fell away for both of them as he kissed her with hungry intensity, his hands holding her so close that she found it difficult to breathe. Passion leaped between them like sparks from two fires. Dinah was weak and helpless in the grip of that burning fever. She had never felt anything like it before. It was a long time before either of them was in a state to say much. Greg reluctantly drew away and groaned.

"I suppose we'd better get home. I'm in no fit state for polite conversation, though."

Dinah was thinking, her brow furrowed. "Sir Gee isn't going to like it, you know, Greg. He won't approve. I'm not exactly a great catch for you, am I?"

"Mother will deal with him," Greg said cheerfully.

"Your faith in your mother is touching," Dinah teased.

"Father may start out by bellowing the house down, but if my mother is on our side we have no problems at all."

They started back down toward Staunton, the blue sky echoing with the song of a lark which was poised high overhead. Dinah gave a deep, contented sigh, her hand held firmly by Greg's powerful fingers.

187

"I knew you were dangerous the minute I set eyes on you."

Greg gave her a mocking grin. "Strange—I was about to say exactly the same thing. We'll be living proof that myths can come true. We'll be able to tell our grandchildren we fell in love at first sight."

"That's not how I remember it," Dinah disputed, laughing.

"By the time we have grandchildren I'll have made you admit it," Greg whispered, his gray eyes gleaming sideways at her. "You fell for me the way I fell for you—at first glance."

"I did not," Dinah argued. "I disliked you the minute I set eyes on you."

"Liar," he teased softly. "It was love at first sight."

"No," Dinah said, laughing.

"Yes," Greg said, laughing back.

She considered him, her blue eyes wide and amused. "Well, maybe just a little." Greg's smile deepened, and Dinah added sweetly, "If that's what you want to believe."

He gave her a wicked, thoughtful look. "I'm beginning to see why my mother thinks so highly of you. Why didn't it strike me before? You're a lot like her in many ways."

Dinah began to laugh, and Greg halted to give her another kiss, his hands framing her laughing face. Above them the closely woven branches of the hazel trees in the spinney whispered together, but neither Greg nor Dinah heard them for a long time.

IT'S YOUR OWN SPECIAL TIME

Contemporary romances for today's women.
Each month, six very special love stories will be yours
from SILHOUETTE.
Look for them wherever books are sold
or order now from the coupon below.

$1.50 each

Silhouette Romance

___ #55 WINTER'S HEART Ladame
___ #56 RISING STAR Trent
___ #57 TO TRUST TOMORROW John
___ #58 LONG WINTER'S NIGHT Stanford
___ #59 KISSED BY MOONLIGHT Vernon
___ #60 GREEN PARADISE Hill
___ #61 WHISPER MY NAME Michaels
___ #62 STAND-IN BRIDE Halston
___ #63 SNOWFLAKES IN THE SUN Brent
___ #64 SHADOW OF APOLLO Hampson
___ #65 A TOUCH OF MAGIC Hunter
___ #66 PROMISES FROM THE PAST Vitek
___ #67 ISLAND CONQUEST Hastings
___ #68 THE MARRIAGE BARGAIN Scott
___ #69 WEST OF THE MOON St. George
___ #70 MADE FOR EACH OTHER Afton Bonds
___ #71 A SECOND CHANCE ON LOVE Ripy
___ #72 ANGRY LOVER Beckman
___ #73 WREN OF PARADISE Browning
___ #74 WINTER DREAMS Trent
___ #75 DIVIDE THE WIND Carroll
___ #76 BURNING MEMORIES Hardy

___ #77 SECRET MARRIAGE Cork
___ #78 DOUBLE OR NOTHING Oliver
___ #79 TO START AGAIN Halldorson
___ #80 WONDER AND WILD DESIRE Stephens
___ #81 IRISH THOROUGHBRED Roberts
___ #82 THE HOSTAGE BRIDE Dailey
___ #83 LOVE LEGACY Halston
___ #84 VEIL OF GOLD Vitek
___ #85 OUTBACK SUMMER John
___ #86 THE MOTH AND THE FLAME Adams
___ #87 BEYOND TOMORROW Michaels
___ #88 AND THEN CAME DAWN Stanford
___ #89 A PASSIONATE BUSINESS James
___ #90 WILD LADY Major
___ #91 WRITTEN IN THE STARS Hunter
___ #92 DESERT DEVIL McKay
___ #93 EAST OF TODAY Browning
___ #94 ENCHANTMENT Hampson
___ #95 FOURTEEN KARAT BEAUTY Wisdom
___ #96 LOVE'S TREACHEROUS JOURNEY Beckman
___ #97 WANDERER'S DREAM Clay
___ #98 MIDNIGHT WINE St. George
___ #99 TO HAVE, TO HOLD Camp

- -

SILHOUETTE BOOKS, Department SB/1
1230 Avenue of the Americas
New York, NY 10020

Please send me the books I have checked above. I am enclosing
$_____ (please add 50¢ to cover postage and handling. NYS and
NYC residents please add appropriate sales tax). Send check or
money order—no cash or C.O.D.'s please. Allow six weeks for delivery.

NAME_____

ADDRESS_____

CITY_____STATE/ZIP_____

Silhouette Romance

15-Day Free Trial Offer
6 Silhouette Romances

6 Silhouette Romances, free for 15 days! We'll send you 6 new Silhouette Romances to keep for 15 days, absolutely free! If you decide not to keep them, send them back to us. You pay nothing.

Free Home Delivery. But if you enjoy them as much as we think you will, keep them by paying the invoice enclosed with your free trial shipment. We'll pay all shipping and handling charges. You get the convenience of Home Delivery and we pay the postage and handling charge each month.

Don't miss a copy. The Silhouette Book Club is the way to make sure you'll be able to receive every new romance we publish before they're sold out. There is no minimum number of books to buy and you can cancel at any time.

This offer expires February 28, 1982

Silhouette Book Club, Dept. **SBG**17B
120 Brighton Road, Clifton, NJ 07012

Please send me 6 Silhouette Romances to keep for 15 days, absolutely free. I understand I am not obligated to join the Silhouette Book Club unless I decide to keep them.

NAME

ADDRESS

CITY_____ STATE_____ ZIP_____

READERS' COMMENTS ON SILHOUETTE ROMANCES:

"Your books are written with so much feeling and quality that they make you feel as if you are part of the story."
—D.C.*, Piedmont, SC

"I'm very particular about the types of romances I read; yours more than fill my thirst for reading."
—C.D., Oxford, MI

"I hope Silhouette novels stay around for many years to come. . . . Keep up the good work."
—P.C., Frederick, MD

"What a relief to be able to escape in a well-written romantic story."
—E.N., Santa Maria, CA

"Silhouette Romances . . . Fantastic!"
—M.D., Bell, CA.

"I'm pleased to be adding your books to my collection—my library is growing in size every day."
—B.L., La Crescenta, CA

* Names available on request.